WEEKLY READER CHILDREN'S BOOK CLUB PRESENTS

EARTH TIMES TWO

EARTH TIMES TWO
PAMELA REYNOLDS

LOTHROP, LEE & SHEPARD CO. ✳ NEW YORK

By the Same Author

A Different Kind of Sister
Horseshoe Hill

To Nora and Brian and Diana

Library of Congress Catalog Card Number: 79-121823

Weekly Reader Children's Book Club Edition
Senior Division

EARTH TIMES TWO

1

Except for the gulls wheeling and calling angrily above him, Jeremy Hillis was alone on the beach. Head lowered, hands deep in the pockets of his jeans, he walked slowly along near the tide line in the direction of the village. His feet dragged more and more until finally he came to a stop and stood staring out over the calm water of the harbor.

On the distant Connecticut shore the sun lay like a neatly halved orange. It was late, past six and probably close to seven. Jeremy had been told to be home by six. He sighed and began walking again.

His "last day of freedom"—that was what his friends had called it. But Jeremy hadn't needed his friends' reminder. After today everything in the Hillis household was going to be different.

Jeremy and his father had lived alone since his mother's death in a sailing accident eight years before. Jeremy had been five then, and although he remembered missing his mother, he didn't really remember much about her. He had never been lonesome. Stony Point University, where his father taught psychology, was only a short distance up the road from their house, so Professor Hillis was able to spend a great deal of time with his son. On the whole they had a fine, casual life together and Jeremy's freedom from female restrictions was the envy of the other boys.

Now, however, a girl was coming to live with them. Not just any girl, but a cousin he didn't even know. Jeremy jammed his hands deeper into the pockets of his jeans. Why couldn't Helene have been a boy? Summer vacation was just starting; he could have had fun with a boy.

The only thing to do was stay out of the house as much as he could. Only that morning, Magda, the Hillises' daily housekeeper, had started making changes. Guinea pigs and gerbils had been ordered out of the living room into the garage. When Jeremy had returned from taking care of that, he'd found the dining room rearranged too. His chemistry experiment was gone from the buffet; chairs and table were placed so that you couldn't watch television while you ate.

Jeremy kicked so fiercely at the sand that a sneaker shot off and flew up into the air. With a sigh, he squatted down to put it back on. As he straightened up, he saw something move beneath the old pier on the beach ahead of him. He looked more closely—and saw nothing. He started walking again, and it reappeared—a flicker of movement, like a star whose twinkle you have caught in the corner of an eye.

He walked faster, keeping his eyes carefully away from the shadows under the pier. Then, very slowly, he allowed his gaze to slide over.

Swirling dots of dark and light filled the shadows. The light dots seemed to be gathering together into a vertical column of some sort . . . a human figure! In his surprise,

8*

Jeremy looked straight at it—and the figure disappeared.

But someone was under the pier. It was probably a trick of the fading light that made the person seem to come and go like that.

Then, when Jeremy was still a good fifty yards away from the pier, he saw it again, as if he were looking through binoculars and someone had twisted the lenses into focus. A girl was standing beneath the pier—a girl with long pale hair, white arms, and long thin legs. She was dressed in a short greenish tunic and stood staring out over the water as if bewitched.

She was about Jeremy's own age, and he felt he should know her. After all, Stony Point was a small village and everyone knew everyone else. In fact, there *was* something vaguely familiar about her. Jeremy frowned, then shook his head. She was no one he had ever seen before.

Suddenly the girl saw him. Her eyes widened and her mouth made a noiseless O of surprise. At the same time, things went out of focus again for Jeremy. Dots of dark and light swirled so quickly around the girl that his eyes ached. Quickly he pressed his hands to them. When he looked again, she was gone.

Seconds later, Jeremy stood panting beneath the pier on the exact spot where the stranger had stood. There was no place here to hide. There was no one in the water, either. He noticed one thing, however: a line of footprints leading from the water to where he stood. They were the tracks of small bare feet, coming in from the wide spread of the outgoing waves—and they did not go back, or sideways, or anywhere at all.

Quickly Jeremy jumped away from the footprints. He wanted to run, but forced himself to stand still and consider the situation in a logical manner. A long row of rocks—a breakwater—extended from the pier out into the water. The girl might have easily jumped from here to the first rock, slipped into the water, and swum out to one of the rowboats anchored near the shore. Jeremy stared into the golden dazzle of the sun track on the water while his heartbeat slowly returned to normal.

Nevertheless, logic dictated relentlessly, girls seldom went into the water with their clothes on, and only an Olympic champion could have managed a standing jump of that magnitude. Still, if he didn't believe that, the girl would have to be a ghost or something, and Jeremy had been in enough trouble when he was little, believing in ghosts and witches and hearing voices that other people didn't hear.

He turned away from the baffling footprints and continued on down the beach. Near the town dock a short flight of steps led to the village square. Jeremy sprinted up the steps, then ran along the sandy path until he came to the open square itself. It consisted of a large area of well-kept grass, dotted here and there with wrought-iron benches. At the center of the square was the Hercules monument. Here, above three graduated tiers of fitted quarry stone, stood the last figurehead from the last whaler to go out from Stony Point early in the nineteenth century. When Jeremy was small he had believed that there was magic in Hercules. He used to make wishes on him, and many times, or so it seemed, the wishes had come true.

He sat down on the lowest step of the monument and stared up at the painted blue eyes. From the University clock tower on the hill came a mellow bong, then another and another—seven altogether. Jeremy stood up. In the excitement about the stranger he had forgotten all about Helene. In fifteen minutes the train from the city would pull into the Stony Point station with his cousin on board.

Jeremy looked up at Hercules and wished. He wished that Helene would not be on that train. Then, right away, he took back the wish—not because he didn't mean it, but because only ten minutes ago he had decided not to have anything to do with any kind of supernatural nonsense.

"In your eye, Herk." He scowled and tossed his gum up at the figurehead. He was not surprised to see it stick in the giant's left eye. It was the sort of luck he often had: good but useless.

The clock was still playing a carillon as Jeremy ran across the square, past the shops on Main Street, and up Quaker Path where he lived. As he turned into his driveway the last note bonged lightly, and then all was still.

Jeremy tiptoed up the back steps and leaned against the house wall next to the kitchen door. Inside he could hear Magda clattering away with the dishes. He was surprised that she didn't hear him, he was puffing so loudly. In a moment or so the clattering stopped and he guessed that she had gone into the dining room. He opened the door and slipped inside. Magda faced him.

"Zo. Von hour late." In moments of stress, her accent was always more noticeable. "Dinner is over. Finished." She made a slicing gesture with one thin hand.

11*

Jeremy noticed that Magda was wearing one of her bright silk Sunday dresses and high heels. Her black hair was sleeked back like a seal's and gold bangles flashed at her ears. Behind her in the dining room he could see his father. *He* was wearing his one good suit.

Professor Hillis frowned at Jeremy, as if he were about to scold him. Then, glancing at his watch, he reconsidered.

"Just run upstairs and get washed, Jeremy. And change something—your shirt perhaps." He surveyed his son dubiously. "Magda, does he or does he not look a trifle grubby?"

Magda rolled her eyes expressively. Putting her hand on Jeremy's neck, she pushed him through the dining room toward the stairs.

"Two minutes," she said, "is all you have."

As Jeremy started up the stairs, his father laid his hand on his arm and looked up at him earnestly for a moment. "We must look our best for Helene," he said. "It's all part of letting her know we want her. She needs that security, Jeremy; you remember how we talked about it."

Jeremy nodded and went on up the stairs. How could he forget? he thought. It was a sad story, and if it hadn't ended with Helene's coming to live with them, he might have felt sorry for her.

It was hard for Jeremy to believe there could have been a woman like his Grandmother Swenson. The bitterness born that day eight years ago, when both her daughters, and Helene's father as well, had been drowned in a sailing accident, had never abated. Professor Hillis had not been with them—and even if he had been, it was not likely he could have saved them. But Mrs. Swenson had blamed him. It was his boat; he was the more experienced sailor. Useless to remind her that the two brothers and the two sisters who had grown up to marry each other had all been competent sailors since childhood. She had never let Helene see her uncle or Jeremy again.

"But there was no room in her life for a child," Jeremy's father had told him. "Her travels, her health, her own interests—they all came first with your grandmother. Helene has never had a real home. She's spent all her life in boarding schools and hotels."

And now Grandmother Swenson was dead, and Helene had been flown home from Europe. Just enough of her grandmother's estate had been left to pay bills at the fancy boarding school in France where she'd been staying.

Jeremy frowned into the mirror as he rubbed at the Good Humor smears around his mouth. He pitied Helene, but he still didn't want her to live with them. Wasn't there somewhere else she could go? Wasn't there someone else, another relative maybe, who would take a thirteen-year-old girl?

"Anyway," he remembered his father saying, "since Helene is my brother's child as well as your mother's sister's child, that means you two have inherited as many of the same genes as a brother and sister. You're double cousins, you might say."

His father had seemed quite pleased with the notion, but Jeremy was appalled. Not just a cousin, but one with a special built-in claim on him!

"Hurry, Jeremy." Magda's scolding tones came floating

up the stairwell. Jeremy threw the washcloth in the sink. He ran across the hall into his room and grabbed a clean shirt from the closet. Then he ran downstairs, buttoning the shirt as he went.

The train from New York was pulling in as they drove up to the station. Professor Hillis jumped out of the car and started across the parking lot toward the platform. Magda followed closely behind him, her thin legs scissoring rapidly across the blacktop.

With a sigh, Jeremy got out of the car too. While his father and Magda paced back and forth next to the slowing train, he sauntered over to the station house and sat down on a bench near the wall.

The train stopped. Up near the front, a large group of people got off: three or four couples carrying vacation-type luggage, a dozen or so boys and girls from the University. From the club car came a troop of wilted-looking commuters. But there was no girl alone, no Helene.

Professor Hillis and Magda were talking to the conductor, Magda waving her hands about excitedly. Jeremy saw the conductor shake his head, then climb back on board the train. It began to move. Jeremy stood up. Was it possible? Had someone else claimed her at the last minute? He made a mental note to take the gum out of Hercules' eye tomorrow.

Suddenly brakes screeched and the train lurched to a second stop. At the door to the end car another conductor appeared, carrying a large canvas bag in one hand and a cardboard box in the other. He beckoned to the Professor.

"Hillis?" he called. When the Professor nodded, the

conductor dropped the canvas bag and the box to the platform and disappeared again in the car. A huge puff of white smoke billowing up from under the wheels temporarily obscured the door. Suddenly from out of the smoke came a battered suitcase and another box.

"Jeremy!" Professor Hillis turned and looked meaningfully at him, and Jeremy stepped forward. He was just in time to receive a large bird cage from the conductor. Inside the cage was a black bird with gold-rimmed eyes.

"Stupid," it said as Jeremy took hold of the handle. He was so startled that he let the cage crash down onto the platform. The black bird went sliding along its perch to bump into the bars at the opposite end. Jeremy bent to pick up the cage and was rewarded by a sharp peck at his fingers. He gave the cage a shake.

A sharp voice rang out from just above him. "Stop that! Do you want to kill him?" Looking up, Jeremy saw a girl step down through the smoke. Long blond hair fell forward, hiding her face.

"I'll take it now," she said crisply, holding out her arms. Smoke wisps danced about her face as she shook back her hair. Jeremy stared at her.

"I said I'll take it," she repeated. But Jeremy's arms refused to move as he continued to stare at his cousin. Helene's face was the face of the girl on the beach.

2

"Helene! How good to see you." Professor Hillis tried to hug the slight figure on the platform, but the bird cage clutched to Helene's chest stopped him. He patted her on the shoulder instead.

"It was kind of you to invite me to visit you, Uncle Bill," Helene said.

The Professor continued to pat her shoulder as he presented her to the others. "Here's your cousin Jeremy. I don't suppose you remember him after so many years. Come on, Jeremy, say hello to Helene."

The Professor frowned as he spoke because Jeremy was still staring blankly at his cousin. She *couldn't* be the girl on the beach. Yet . . . how could two people look so exactly alike?

"Jeremy?"

Finally his father's voice prompted him into speech. "Hi," Jeremy mumbled.

"How do you do?" Helene articulated clearly, a smile twitching briefly at her lips.

"And this . . . this is Mrs. Dachenhausen," Professor Hillis continued, stumbling over the name. It had been years since he and Jeremy had used it.

No one had to pull Magda forward. With a little rush

she came up on the other side of Helene and kissed her cheek.

"Magda, call me Magda, darling," she told her. "Here, you look tired. Let me take this." Magda put her hand on the bird cage.

"No!" Helene's voice was sharp. She added quickly, "Thank you, but I can manage, Mrs. Dachenhausen." Her white-gloved hand tightened on the cage.

"Well then, let's go," the Professor said. He distributed the rest of the luggage between himself and Jeremy, and they started back across the parking lot toward the car.

"For a minute there, I thought you'd missed the train, Helene," he said as he drove the car down the hill toward the village. "Had me worried," he added, tipping his head to grin at her in the mirror.

"I'm terribly sorry if I worried you, Uncle Bill," said Helene, trilling her *R*'s. "I had to be careful with Teddy when the train stopped. He can't stand being shaken up in any way." She placed a protective hand on the bird cage and gave Jeremy a poisonous look.

Turning away from her, Jeremy stared glumly out the window as the familiar streets of the village came into sight. Helene was rapidly turning out to be the kind of girl he despised.

Professor Hillis began pointing out places of interest to Helene. "That's the Whaling Museum," he said. "And now you can see the harbor. One of the safest in the world. That's because of those two arms of land that come out on either side and almost enclose it. There's the lighthouse on one arm and Old Fort on the other. We'll take you to

17*

visit Old Fort soon; it's interesting. Jeremy can show you all the secret stairways and hiding places."

"They've raised the price. Costs a dollar apiece to get in now," Jeremy said. The last thing he wanted to do was drag his cousin around the fort with him. Helene shot him another mean-eyed look as if to say that *she*, at least, knew what he meant, even though the two adults up front seemed oblivious.

"And see the flowers!" Magda pointed excitedly at the baskets of geraniums and ivy hanging from the old-fashioned lampposts. "They are *new*. That is because we are restored here in Stony Point," she added proudly.

Jeremy watched his cousin covertly as Magda chattered away in the front seat about the restoration of the town. Helene never raised her eyes from the myna bird's cage. "How perfectly delightful," she murmured. "How quaint." Jeremy edged away from her. What a phoney. He couldn't wait to get home so that he could escape.

When they drove up to the little white house on Quaker Path, the Professor stopped the car before they reached the driveway. He pointed to a brass plaque above the front door.

"Sixteen eighty-seven," he said proudly. "One of the oldest houses around here."

Inside the house the colonial influence was evident. The rooms were tiny, the fireplaces huge. The antiques Jeremy's mother had chosen years ago blended well with the few comfortable upholstered pieces. Jeremy was used to hearing visitors exclaim over the charm of the place, but today he tried to look at it through Helene's eyes. Her perfunctory "How quaint" was all he had to hear. Coming from a fancy school in Europe the way she had, maybe everything just looked worn out to Helene. Maybe she didn't know it was all supposed to look old.

Jeremy dumped the suitcases onto the floor of the upstairs bedroom that would be Helene's. Then while the others were getting things settled, he slipped out. But just as he reached the foot of the stairs his father called him. He stopped and waited as the Professor came hurrying down.

"I hope you weren't thinking of going out again," he said in a low voice. "It's up to you more than anyone else to make Helene feel at home here." He clapped his hand on Jeremy's shoulder. "It's so important, so important. We're all she has now, and she mustn't feel rejected." His face was serious.

"OK," Jeremy sighed. "Sure." He wasn't unkind. Despite his initial resentment of his cousin, Jeremy's sense of fair play would have forced him to cooperate with his father. Except for one thing. Helene had made it very clear right from the first moment that she didn't like *him*.

"Tell you what," the Professor went on, "we'll have a fire. That always makes a place seem cozy—and there's a chill tonight. You get it started, Jeremy, while I go out back for some logs." Another friendly clap on Jeremy's shoulder, and he was gone.

Jeremy wandered over to the television set. Maybe there was something good on. Then he wouldn't have to talk to Helene.

His hand was on the switch when a voice whispered piercingly in his ear. "Is not friendly to watch television." Magda had come up behind him in her Indian-footed way, and as Jeremy turned around, her black eyes bore into his. She jerked her head toward the hall, where footsteps could be heard on the stairs. "Be nice," she hissed.

Helene entered the room, carrying the bird cage. "Teddy's very upset," she said, looking at Magda and ignoring Jeremy. "The train ride was bad for him."

Magda clucked sympathetically and guided Helene to one of the comfortable wing chairs near the fireplace. "Sit and rest," she said. "I'll get you a little snack." She beamed down at Helene for a second longer and then went into the kitchen. Jeremy was left alone with his cousin.

"Uh . . . I'll start the fire," he muttered, kneeling down and pulling papers and kindling from the wood-box.

In a moment flames from the papers blazed up and Jeremy backed away, bumping into the bird cage as he did so. Helene made a little sound of annoyance and Jeremy looked at her. With the firelight gilding her hair and skin like the glow of the sunset, she looked more than ever like the girl on the beach. He felt the hair on his neck prickle.

Helene narrowed her eyes. "Didn't anyone ever tell you it's not polite to stare?" she asked. Jeremy's face got hot, but before he could think of an appropriate reply, his father came back into the room with the logs.

For the next few minutes they were busy building up the fire. When at last Jeremy sat back in the other wing chair opposite Helene, his eyes were drawn again to her face. In an instant, her eyes met his. Jeremy looked away. He hoped she didn't think he was looking at her because he liked her or anything like that. The truth was, he found

Helene interesting, the same way he found a snake or a black-widow spider interesting. Then, too, the feeling that she was in some way connected with the mysterious girl on the beach gave her a certain fascination. But as for being "nice" to his cousin! The spider image took over again, and Jeremy's mind backed away.

"Well, now." Jeremy looked up to see his father watching them. "How about a game or something? Get the Monopoly or the Scrabble, Jeremy."

Jeremy got up and went over to the bookcase where the games were. He had already pulled out the Monopoly when he noticed a deck of cards lying on the shelf below. Of course, he thought, with the first feeling of satisfaction he'd experienced since Helene's arrival, they'd play cards. That was the way to wipe that superior look off Helene's face. His fingers closed tightly around the familiar shape of the card case.

He hurried back to the fireplace. Pulling a hassock out from under his chair to make a table between them, he said to his cousin, "How about gin rummy?" He tried to sound casual.

"All right." Helene's tone matched his.

They began to play. It was only a question of time, Jeremy thought confidently. He would single out a few cards to build into sets and then, very soon, he would find matching cards. *It* would help him.

Jeremy had never tried to define, even to himself, exactly what *it* was. He only knew that, if he concentrated, he could tell what a card was without looking at its face. Oh, once in a while he made mistakes, but usually a picture—or was it a feeling?—of the card came through to

21*

him clearly. *It* worked so well that sometimes Jeremy had to pretend to lose to avoid the charge of cheating.

Now, as he looked over his hand, he decided that he would save fives and tens and Jacks. Since he was dealer, he went first. Reaching out his hand to the draw pack, he hesitated. What was the card? Did he want it—or was the one on the discard pile more suited to his hand? What *was* the card? Jeremy waited for the feeling to come. But there was nothing. He concentrated harder.

"Ho hum!" Helene patted back an imaginary yawn.

Jeremy quickly picked up the top card and jammed it into his hand. It was not one he needed.

Helene played the game swiftly. That only seemed to point up Jeremy's slowness as he waited for *it* to start operating. He began to hate the sight of Helene's skinny little fingers flying back and forth from the draw deck to her hand. Her fingernails were bitten to the quick, and their raw, red look disgusted him. But he couldn't look away.

What is the card, what is it? he thought desperately each time he held his hand over the draw pack. At last, when the game had been in progress for some fifteen minutes, a glimmer began to come through . . . just a glimmer.

A sudden rustle and squawking in the bird cage next to him broke up Jeremy's train of thought. "My nerves, my nerves!" screamed the myna, sounding just like a querulous old lady. "Go to your room! Go to your room!"

Jeremy heard Helene draw in her breath with a funny little sound, almost like a sob. Then she bent and tapped softly on the bars of the cage. Teddy ruffled his feathers and rubbed his head against Helene's fingers before settling back into silence. But the feeling was gone now for Jeremy—if it had ever been there at all. He sighed and picked up the top card, not at all surprised to find that it was another wrong one.

Then the blow fell. "Gin," Helene announced calmly. She spread three Jacks, three tens, and a run of diamonds onto the hassock.

"I'm afraid I've beaten you, Jeremy," she said sweetly.

The Professor put down his newspaper. "What? Beaten the old card shark?" He got up and walked over to them. "No one ever beats him, Helene. Didn't he tell you he has second sight with cards?" He chuckled, oblivious to Jeremy's warning glance. "Do you know, Helene, that when Jeremy was small he really thought it was something like that. I must admit he's unusually lucky. But that's all it is. I'm not one of those psychologists who go along with ESP and so forth. Do you know what else he believed when he was little?" The Professor settled himself on the hearth rug and wrapped his arms around his knees.

Jeremy cringed as he saw Helene lean forward, a malicious look in her eyes. He wondered if he should fall into the fire to create a diversion, and had just about made up his mind to do it when Magda appeared in the kitchen doorway with a large tray in her hands.

"Twints," she announced loudly, nodding first toward Helene and then toward Jeremy. "They look like twints."

"Twins!" Jeremy couldn't keep the distaste from his voice. Looking like any girl would be bad, but having someone say he resembled Helene was terrible.

"It's true in a way," the Professor said. "It shouldn't surprise you, Jeremy. I told you you were double cousins."

"Keep letting the hair grow and you look even *more*," Magda said, waving the cake knife in Jeremy's direction.

Jeremy's lips tightened. It wasn't fair to bring that up now—especially in front of Helene.

"You will look like her *Doppelgänger* soon," Magda went on.

Jeremy quickly seized on the word. *"Doppelgänger? Doppelgänger?* What's that?"

"Your double, someone who looks just like you," Magda answered. "Come, have a nice piece of strudel," she coaxed Helene.

Helene ignored the proffered plate. "Does everyone have a . . . *Doppelgänger?"* she asked, her eyes fastened on Magda's.

"No, of course not. Maybe nobody does. Is just a story. Come, eat."

"Tell it, tell the story," Jeremy urged. Much of his exasperation had diminished when he started eating the apple cake. Having had no dinner, he found it tasted doubly delicious. One of Magda's stories about the "old country" would go well with it.

"Not much to tell." Magda shrugged. "There was a man in our village, my mother told me, who saw himself, his *Doppelgänger.* First he saw him walking in the field where they were mowing. Then another day he saw him on the road when he was taking his milk into town. And then, one day, he saw the *Doppelgänger* going into his own house. And the man ran up to stop him. He reached out his hand to lay it on the *Doppelgänger's* arm and then. . . ." Magda paused dramatically. "Poof! They both disappeared."

24*

"Keen," Jeremy said, licking sugar from his fingers. "But isn't there any more to the story? Like what is a *Doppelgänger* and all that?"

"Is story only I told you. Anyhow, it brings bad luck to speak of it."

Jeremy hooted. "First you say it's not true and then you say it brings bad luck. It can't be both."

Magda set her lips in a thin line as she sliced another piece of strudel for the Professor. She was obviously finished with the subject.

The Professor was not. Jeremy could tell by the way he leaned forward, pulling on his ear, that he was about to lecture.

"It's interesting, you know. Psychology borrowed the word *Doppelgänger* to describe a certain type of hallucinatory disturbance. Hallucination: from the Latin *hallucinare,* to wander mentally. You should know that, Jeremy. An hallucination, therefore, is the perception of a sight or sound not actually present." The Professor took another bite of strudel.

But what's a *Doppelgänger*, Jeremy wanted to ask. He shifted restlessly about in his chair, glancing over at Helene as he did so. She wasn't the least bit bored by all the psychological jargon, but was leaning forward with an intense look on her face.

"Go on, Uncle Bill," she urged.

The Professor smiled at her in a pleased way. "Well," he said, "people who hallucinate and see themselves, rather than, say, little pink men from Mars, are said to have a *Doppelgänger* response. Usually this other self, or mirror image, is doing something the person in question would

25*

like to do but cannot, due to some psychic block. Therefore, Magda," he concluded with the air of someone pulling a rabbit out of a hat, "you certainly could say that to see a *Doppelgänger* brings bad luck. Someone with a personality disorder of such magnitude would be mixed-up and unhappy to say the least."

Helene's eyes searched his face. "Why does this happen, Uncle Bill? Why would it seem so real that a person would think she could touch her *Doppelgänger?*"

Jeremy could see his father was ready to go on for hours about personality disorders and such, throwing the more interesting discussion of *Doppelgängers*-who-go-poof right out the window.

"You mean the whole thing is just psychological? There really aren't any *Doppelgängers?*" he asked.

His father laughed. "Oh, come now, Jeremy, I believe you still like to scare yourself." He turned to Helene. "If you knew all the things this boy tried to believe in when he was a little fellow: ghosts and goblins and things that go bump in the night." He shook his head. Helene looked at Jeremy with an odd smile.

"You needn't laugh," Jeremy told them all sourly. "For your information, I've even seen a *Doppelgänger*. Hers." He pointed to Helene. "That's right, I saw your *Doppelgänger* right down on the Stony Point beach tonight."

This time the sound of Helene's indrawn breath was clearly audible to everyone, and Jeremy saw Magda and his father exchange a puzzled look. His own reaction was mainly one of satisfaction at seeing the withdrawn, superior expression disappear from his cousin's face.

He continued. "She was exactly like you, exactly." He

then described the girl's mysterious appearance and disappearance beneath the pier. He even told about the swirling mist that had surrounded her and the way it shimmered with bits of light and dark. As he talked, the sense of unreality he'd had on the beach returned.

"And there were these footprints. . . ." His voice died out. Nothing, no coincidence or trick of the fading sunlight, could explain away those footprints that began and ended in nowhere. The prickle of fear came back and suddenly Jeremy didn't want to talk about *Doppelgängers* anymore.

Helene continued to stare at him with big eyes. Jeremy realized that she hadn't blinked all the time he'd been talking.

The Professor stood up suddenly. "I think we've had enough ghost stories for tonight," he said.

Magda stood up too. "Is time for everyone to go to bed," she announced, looking at Jeremy. He heard her low-voiced aside to the Professor: "She is very tired. See how pale she is."

The fire had died down and, in the flickering light that remained, Helene looked so white that the shadows beneath her eyes might have been painted on. Huddled down in the big chair she looked very small—weak, somehow. Jeremy felt a pang of remorse.

For some time now, he had been aware of small movements back in the shadows of the woodbox. He knew it was Charlie, his cat, and now, as a striped head and shoulders appeared, he jumped up. Charlie was looking at Helene in an interested way. Jeremy stepped aside so that she could see him.

"Here's Charlie," he said proudly, but was cut off short by Helene's cry of alarm. With a scramble of skinny arms and legs she dropped to the floor in front of the bird cage.

"Oh, please, get the cat out of here," she cried. "Teddy is so afraid of cats!"

Jeremy's private opinion of Teddy was that he was equal to any cat alive—or dog for that matter—but by now the Professor and Magda were crouching down on the floor too, trying to comfort Helene, and there was nothing for him to do but scoop Charlie up in his arms. He started for the stairs.

"Outside with the cat," his father ordered.

"I'm taking him to my room," Jeremy said.

The Professor shook his head. "Not tonight," he said. "Outside. All the way."

That wasn't fair. His father knew that Charlie always slept with Jeremy, had done so since he was a kitten. But Helene was crying softly now, and one look at his father's face warned Jeremy not to argue. He walked slowly out of the room.

He released Charlie on the back porch, then stood there for a moment letting the breeze from the harbor cool his hot cheeks. There was a smell of salt in the wind, and tar, and a pungent fishy smell of low tide. It felt good to be out here, away from Helene's prickly presence.

Charlie moved off into the darkness without a backward glance. Maybe he wouldn't mind sleeping outside, Jeremy thought. Maybe cats didn't care that much about people anyway. Jeremy sighed as he turned back to the house. He knew *he'd* be lonesome tonight.

28*

3

A long time passed before Jeremy got to sleep that night. Thoughts kept popping into his head like sparks and made him toss and turn restlessly. Who was the girl on the beach? What was her connection with Helene? After a while another thought kept returning with disturbing insistency: where was Charlie? Perhaps he had run away. The bed felt so strange without the cat's firm round shape to curl around. Jeremy punched the pillow a few more times, then balled it up against his chest. In that way he finally fell asleep.

It seemed to him that he'd hardly slept at all when there was a knock at the door. Lifting his head, he stared groggily toward the sound. His room was still night-black, but a pencil line of brightness around the door frame came from a light in the hall.

The door opened. Jeremy squinted up to see his father's head and shoulders silhouetted against the light.

"What is it?" he mumbled.

"Listen, Jeremy, last night when Captain Harry came to pick up Magda, he brought a pail of bait . . . and some news!" The Professor was trying to whisper but now his voice started to rise.

"Snappers!" Jeremy was suddenly wide awake.

"The tide turns at six. Can you be ready?"

"You bet!" Jeremy jumped out of bed as the door closed softly and his father's steps receded down the hall.

He'd known it was time for snappers, he thought happily as he stumbled across the room toward the light switch. All the boys in the village had been speculating for weeks about when the tide would wash in that first enormous, wonderful army of fish. No one was ever very sure about it—except Captain Harry Dachenhausen.

In the little house near the pier, which was bait shack and home for him and Magda, Captain Harry was very close to the tides and to the comings and goings of all sorts of marine life. He was always able to foretell the day the snappers were coming—and he always told his old friend Professor Hillis. Thanks to the Captain, Jeremy and his father had fished the first snapper run for many years. The summer never really began for Jeremy until then.

He ran down the stairs two at a time, heading for the lighted kitchen. His father was at the stove making coffee. On the table was the old brown wicker picnic basket, already packed and covered by the red-and-white checked tablecloth they always took with them.

As Jeremy came into the room, he caught his father's eye and grinned. "I'll get the gear," he said, not breaking stride as he went on out the back door into the blackness of the yard. Enough light from the kitchen window shone fuzzily through the heavy fog to guide him to the garage. He slipped through the half-opened door and switched on the light.

Inside the garage Jeremy began poking through the assortment of brooms, shovels, and curtain rods stacked against the wall until he located the fishing rods. Farther back in the garage an excited squeaking began as the guinea pigs and gerbils awoke. Thrusting his fingers through the cage bars, Jeremy let the little creatures nibble on his fingernails until it occurred to him that in all the fuss the night before he had forgotten to feed them.

It took him a few minutes to find the bag of pellets and measure them into the feeding cups. By the time he had replenished the water bottles, too, it was beginning to get a bit light outside. He'd better hurry and get the hooks and sinkers together. Luckily they were right where they were supposed to be, and near them, cozily ensconced on a coil of rope, was Charlie. Relief swept over Jeremy. Now the day would be perfect.

He bent down until his cheek touched the cat's furry back. "Wake up," he said, although Charlie wasn't asleep any more than a cat ever was. Jeremy waved the fishy-smelling box of hooks under Charlie's nose.

Charlie rose, stretched, and jumped to the floor. He began weaving himself around Jeremy's ankles.

Jeremy regarded him fondly. "Come on," he said, and started back toward the house.

On the back step, Jeremy stopped. Voices in the kitchen? That wasn't right. He went slowly up the steps. When he opened the kitchen door he saw Helene standing next to his father near the stove. They were laughing together, Helene looking unexpectedly animated. Jeremy looked from one to the other. There was no need of Helene's pert "I'm going too," to apprise him of the situation. He sat down heavily in one of the kitchen chairs.

Helene looked as if she were going to a party. She was

31*

wearing a short white dress with fanlike pleats ending high above her skinny knees. White arms, white legs, white dress—to Jeremy she looked like some unhealthy kind of grub.

"Are you going to wear *that*?" he asked.

The Professor put his arm around Helene's shoulders and smiled down at her.

"You know what? I tiptoed into Helene's room—*very* quietly, I thought—to leave a note about our going, and there she was, sitting up wide awake . . . looking just a bit scared." The Professor's eyes met Jeremy's. "So, of *course,* I invited her to come with us. But you can still change your mind, Helene," he added. "Magda will be here in an hour or so. You could go back to bed and sleep until noon if you wanted to."

Helene shook her head. "Oh, no, Uncle Bill," she said. "I want to go with you."

"Or . . . if you don't want to be alone, we could wait until Magda arrives," the Professor went on solicitously. "I mean, being out on the Sound at this hour isn't everybody's cup of tea."

Helene shook her head again.

Jeremy jumped up, scattering the box of fishhooks onto the floor. He was willing to accept the fact that his father had no choice but to invite Helene. However, his latest offer to waste several hours of valuable morning time seemed unfair. The whole point of knowing about the snappers was to be there when the tide turned.

"Let's eat," he said. "It's getting late."

Breakfast took twice as long as usual and even then,

when it was over, Helene had to go back to her room for a sweater. Then the Professor couldn't find his glasses. Then Helene had to run upstairs once more to see if she had uncovered Teddy. Jeremy finally went out onto the back porch to wait, hoping that would speed things up.

Charlie sat next to the fishing gear and Jeremy bent down to stroke him. He'd be willing to bet that Helene wouldn't say anything about Charlie's going on the boat with them. She'd probably pretend that it was a very ordinary thing for a cat to do. He straightened up and began flicking the flashlight beam around the yard, noticing how the heavy fog shortened and dispersed the beam.

"Shine that over here, Jeremy," the Professor said as he came out the door. He had the picnic basket on one arm and Helene on the other. Helene clung to her uncle, casting apprehensive looks at the fog-filled shadows. Coming down the steps, she tripped, and from then on Jeremy kept the flashlight beam close to her feet. He didn't care if she fell—but it would cause more delay.

Out on the road it was somewhat lighter although the flashlight still penetrated only a few yards into the fog. Along the side of the road deeper shadows indicated trees and houses. It was very quiet; their footsteps, loud and scratchy on the dirt road, were the only sounds. Suddenly an urgent whisper from Helene drew them to a halt.

"Stop!" she cried.

"What is it?" the Professor asked.

"I heard footsteps. Someone is following us!"

Jeremy shone the light behind them and then all around on either side. No one was there.

33*

"Come on," he said impatiently.

"No, listen. . . . Can't you hear it now?"

He did hear it—a scrabbling sound, regular in rhythm, and coming closer. He knew exactly what it was, and yet he was suddenly overwhelmed with fear. It was the strangest sort of fear, for there was nothing to pin it on, nothing to cause it. Nevertheless, there it was, tightening up his stomach, and making his heart thump wildly. He couldn't even tell Helene what the sound meant because of the dryness of his mouth.

"Look," he heard his father say, "it's only the seagoing cat." As he spoke, Charlie walked into the flashlight beam.

As suddenly as it had come, the fear left Jeremy. He looked about him wonderingly. He'd known all along it was Charlie. Why had that unaccountable panic seized him? As they continued on down the road toward the harbor, he turned it over in his head. Was the fear perhaps left over from a dream last night? No, it would have had to be a *nightmare,* and surely he would have remembered that. It was all very baffling, and for some reason he wanted to blame it on Helene.

In the village the darkened store fronts gave no hint of their identities, except for the Post Office where the lights were always on. In its subdued light Jeremy was able to watch Charlie's antics. He was weaving himself in and out between Helene's ankles, much to her obvious distaste. Jeremy had seen Charlie act that way before. Just give him a real cat-hater and he made every effort to get cozy. Jeremy had never been able to decide whether he did it to annoy or to charm.

As they crossed the parking lot in front of the pier, Helene stopped again. "I can hear waves," she said.

"That's right," the Professor replied cheerfully, "we're almost there now. The boat is out at the end of the dock."

"But—we can hardly see," Helene protested. "Suppose we fall in?"

Jeremy laughed. "We know where we are," he said.

Just the same, as they made their way out onto the pier, he was glad it was getting lighter. The wide-spaced boards beneath their feet were sturdy enough, but it would be easy to miss your footing, slide between them, and get a nasty scrape on the ankle. He kept the light shining steadily downward as the Professor guided Helene along. On both sides of them the water was inky-black beneath the layer of fog. When the blackness stretched out in front of them too, they knew they had reached the end. There they stopped.

The Professor put the picnic basket and the bait pail down on the pier. Then he walked a few steps, turned around, and began letting himself over the side. Jeremy saw Helene start forward too.

"Where's he going?" she cried.

"Just down onto the float." The Professor paused with his head and shoulders above the edge of the pier. He reached for the basket and the pail. "You're next," he told Helene, and disappeared. Helene pulled her sweater more closely around her shoulders. She didn't move.

"Ho hum." Jeremy yawned elaborately.

Helene's chin went up and she started forward. Without a word or a glance at him she started down the ladder.

When she had disappeared, it was Jeremy's turn. He tightened his arm around the fishing rods and started down. When his shoulders were level with the pier he called to Charlie, and waited patiently while the cat crossed the five feet of pier in a slow, circuitous fashion and finally placed himself precariously on Jeremy's shoulders. It was the part of the trip Charlie disliked most, and his grip on Jeremy tightened as they went down the ladder.

Helene and the Professor were already in the little rowboat tied to the float. Helene sat in the stern, her white skirt gathered about her, her feet planted primly on the boat seam. Jeremy guessed that a dirty old rowboat was not exactly what she'd had in mind when she got herself dressed up in that fancy outfit. He jumped into the boat with an extra flourish and was gratified to see Helene's hands fly out to grip the sides as the boat rocked violently back and forth.

Charlie waited until the boat settled down again before joining them. Then he leaped forward, making a neat four-point landing in the prow.

Jeremy and his father sat side by side in the center seat. Fitting the oars into the locks, they pushed away from the float. As they moved out into the calm waters of the harbor, the mustardy-yellow fog swirled and lifted about them. Pier and float were soon lost to view, but a pocket of open space continued to surround the boat. In order to avoid other craft in the harbor they had to work the oars skillfully each time an anchor rope drifted into the perimeter of their vision. It was almost like other years—almost, but not quite. Jeremy pulled angrily at his oar.

"Easy on," his father cautioned as the boat swung sharply to the right. "Keep it straight. We're going into the channel."

A muffled clanging was heard up ahead. It repeated itself at irregular intervals, growing louder as they moved on. Helene's eyes flew questioningly to her uncle's face.

"That's the bell on the channel marker," he told her. "It means we're getting closer to where all those little fishes are. You see, Helene, the buoy is in the deepest part of the channel, and that's where the tide will be the strongest. . . ." He went on, explaining in detail the spawning habits of the bluefish. At first Helene listened attentively, and then her gaze shifted to a point beyond him, up ahead in the fog.

Jeremy, facing in the opposite direction, wondered what she saw up ahead. He would have turned around to see for himself, but found that he could not take his eyes off Helene's face. It wore a look of disbelief which, as he watched, swiftly turned to one of terror. And then, just at the moment when Helene's mouth dropped open in a soundless· scream, Jeremy felt it again—the *fear*. But the fear that had touched him on the road was mild compared to the wave of panic that washed over him now. He shut his eyes and clung to the oar, unable to lift it.

"Come on, Jeremy," his father cried, "don't stop rowing, the current's getting strong." He spoke sharply, but Jeremy didn't answer. Head down, he was fighting a rising vertigo. The Professor turned around.

"Watch it," he cried, "here comes the buoy!" He pulled hard on his own oar and swung the boat out of the way just in time. The bottle-shaped buoy, tall as a man, sailed past them.

"That was close." The Professor shook his head. "Sort of scary the way it came up like that. Looked like someone walking on the water, didn't it, Helene?"

She murmured something in reply, but Jeremy was hardly aware of it, he was so busy examining what had happened inside himself. When the buoy had appeared, the fear, the unaccountable fear that had nothing to do with his own feelings, had suddenly left him. It was just the way he had felt out on the road.

"We'll anchor here at the edge of the current," the Professor announced, frowning at the rapidly churning waves. "Then we won't be dragged in toward shore. Backwater a little now, Jeremy."

Jeremy followed directions automatically, his head still spinning. He looked up at his cousin. Her face was calm and unreadable again. The fear had left her. Then Jeremy understood. In some dreadful way that he had no control over, there was a link between Helene's mind and his own. The fear he had felt hadn't been his at all. It had been Helene's.

4

No sooner had they stopped rowing and dropped anchor
than the fog settled down around the boat again. However, it was much lighter now and shiny flecks of light
danced in its swirls. Somewhere up above the fog Jeremy
knew that the sun was shining. It would be a hot day—a
great day for fishing on the Sound.

Everything was ordinary—much the way it always was
—but he hadn't imagined the fear, either, · he knew he
hadn't. Jeremy resisted the impulse to stare at his cousin's
face, keeping his eyes riveted on her feet on the floor of
the boat. He didn't move.

"There," the Professor said as he passed a drop line to
Helene. He stood up and moved cautiously to the prow
of the boat. "Move over, cat," he said, and settled himself
next to Charlie. "You know, Helene," he went on, "your
parents used to fish out here with Jeremy's mother and me,
just like this. Your mother used a drop line—like the one
you have. She always caught more fish than any of us."

"She did?" Helene sounded as if she were smiling.
Jeremy looked up. Yes, her pale lips were actually turning
upward a little bit as she stared down at the piece of string
in her hand. For a moment she looked just like any ordinary
girl. But if there was nothing wrong with her, then there

was something very wrong with him. Jeremy groaned.

"What's the matter, Jeremy?" asked his father.

"Uh, nothing." Jeremy quickly picked up his fishing pole. To cover his confusion at having let the sound escape him, he became very busy with the bait and floats and sinkers. He even baited up Helene's line for her, and in a few moments their floats were bobbing on the waves.

Jeremy's sank first.

"Got one! Got one!" he cried, reeling in his line. A silver fish twirled through the air. He caught three more before Helene and his father had any success, and for a while his satisfaction blotted out all other feelings. It was the sort of fishing a boy dreamed about, too easy for a real sportsman perhaps, but highly satisfactory for someone who sometimes sat for hours on the pier without even getting a nibble. One after another the snappers came in. In an hour several dozen fish lay in the net on the bottom of the boat.

"That's it, I think," the Professor said, reeling in his line.

"You mean we're through?" Helene asked. Jeremy thought she sounded relieved.

"For a while," the Professor said. He began hauling up the anchor. "You see, Helene, we catch these particular fish for a special purpose—a special purpose" . . . hand over hand he pulled in the rope . . . "that you will shortly enjoy."

After he and Jeremy were settled back in their rowing positions, the Professor resumed his conversation with Helene.

"We have a little ceremony with these fish, the first snappers of the season. You could almost say it was a sacrifice." He paused. "Yes . . . there might be some sort of racial memory involved—or would it be a cultural indoctrination? . . ." His voice trailed off as he gazed thoughtfully off into the fog.

Jeremy picked up the conversation. "We have a picnic breakfast with these fish—on the island. Then afterward, we come back and catch a whole lot more to take home."

Jeremy wasn't sure what part of the day he liked best: the fishing, the picnic, or giving away the fish to his friends later on. Luckily there was no need to choose; on this day there were enough snappers in the channel to feed all of Stony Point, although most of them, of course, had to be allowed to grow into big bluefish.

A small wind came up now, blowing the fog about until here and there patches of open water showed. These open spaces grew until suddenly they were rowing in full sunlight with the Sound crinkling brilliantly all around them.

"Ahead of us, that shoreline you can see, that's Connecticut," the Professor said, half turning to nod at the low-lying purple hills in the far distance. Helene turned around to look. Just ahead of them lay half a dozen small islands. Two were just large enough for a house and barn; one had a windmill on it; the rest were nothing more than outcroppings of rock covered with scrub pine and dune grass.

It was toward the smallest of these outcroppings that they headed—Pig Island. They had never taken anyone else there before, Jeremy thought. No one ever bothered with Pig Island, except to remark sometimes that a long time ago wild pigs had inhabited it. Braceleted with tall jagged rocks and showing no beach area at all, it was not an inviting spot.

The secret of Pig Island was this: it *had* a beach and there was a way to get to it. Years before, Captain Harry and Jeremy's father had found an opening in the rocks just wide enough for a rowboat to slip through. Within the circle of rocks, not visible from the water, was a narrow pebbly beach.

A few moments more, and the Professor and Jeremy stopped rowing. Using their oars to pole with, they began maneuvering the boat carefully between the barnacle-covered boulders. Helene sat very still in the stern, holding onto the sides of the boat with both hands. In the prow Charlie was equally tense, leaning forward with the wind filling his ears.

"A bit to the left," the Professor whispered. Jeremy held his oar steady. Sweat ran down in front of his eyes as with a grating crunch they slid through the rocks and onto the pebbles.

Charlie uncoiled like a spring and hurled himself over the shallows onto the beach. The others followed more slowly, Jeremy going first with the heavy anchor clutched to his chest. By the time he had hooked it securely in the twisted roots of one of the scraggly pine trees, his father and Helene were on shore too. Anxious to put down the net of still struggling fish, the Professor ran on ahead.

"Help Helene with the basket, Jeremy, will you?" he called back over his shoulder.

That meant "Carry it." Jeremy slowly walked back to where his cousin waited at the shoreline. In crossing through the shallows she had managed to get her white skirt wet and now she stood flapping it against her legs. As Jeremy came up to her she shivered and made a face.

"What a queer place," she said.

Jeremy stopped. "Queer how?" he asked, hooking his thumbs in the belt of his jeans and narrowing his eyes in what he hoped was an intimidating manner.

Helene shrugged. "I don't know," she said. "Those trees" . . . she looked at the stunted pines . . . "do they grow dead or something?"

It wasn't really a stupid remark. Jeremy himself had often wondered why the little pines continued to grow since their foliage was about ninety percent brown. However, Helene shouldn't have made it. He scowled at her, then quoted Captain Harry.

"Scrub pines have guts," he said.

Helene looked skeptical so Jeremy added something else. "At least *they* belong here."

For a second Helene's eyes darkened; then her chin came up and she stalked stiffly across the beach toward her uncle. Jeremy followed her. At the campsite, a circle of blackened stones marked picnics of former years. He dumped the basket onto the ground and walked away. Digging his heels deep into the pebbles, he headed for the end of the island.

"Where to, Jeremy?" his father called.

"To get some wood," Jeremy answered without looking back. There was really no need to go all the way down to

43*

the end for it, but at that moment he just wanted to get away from Helene. As a matter of fact, he would have liked to have escaped from himself then too. That last remark to his cousin had been uncalled for. But after all, he'd gone to help her and she had had to make a snippy remark about the pine trees. He just didn't *like* her, that was all. He walked on, kicking up pebbles as he went. He didn't want to admit, even to himself, that fear of Helene was mixed with his dislike.

Pig Island was so small that it took only a few minutes to reach the end of it, where a natural jetty of rocks stuck out into the water. It was an impossible place to land a boat, and the wind, coming from several directions at the same time, made it useless as a campsite. Yet it was Jeremy's favorite spot on the island.

Through some trick of the merging currents the narrow promontory was a rich depository for jingle shells. Petal-thin, they lay in heaps of frosted pink and gold and silver all along the tide line and sparkled in the crevices of the rocks. Jeremy had never taken any shells. It was enough to know that they were there and *his*. He sat down on the beach and let a handful chime through his fingers. Then he thought about what had happened on the boat, and his mind became confused. Was that what it meant to go crazy? he wondered. He sat there a little longer, playing with the shells, and then stood up. You couldn't solve a problem by running away from it . . . even when you weren't sure what the problem was.

On the way back to the campsite he picked up some driftwood for the fire. A smell of smoke from across the beach told him it was already started, and he walked faster. Soon he could see his father and Helene standing next to a good-sized blaze. Charlie was at their feet. As he came up to them Jeremy saw that the cat was well into his first fish.

Jeremy dumped the wood onto the beach. Potatoes were already roasting, sending forth an appetizing aroma.

"Are the fish ready?" he asked his father.

"Well, you disappeared just in time to avoid gutting them," his father told him. He didn't seem angry, however, but turned to Helene with a smile. "We have a real outdoor cook here, Jeremy. Just like her mother. She learned how to clean those fish in no time at all."

Helene moved closed to her uncle. "Shall I put the butter in the pan now, Uncle Bill?" she asked. When he nodded she dropped a big lump of butter in the skillet and placed it over the fire. When it began to sizzle and turn brown, she added six snappers, picking them up daintily by their tails and laying them in a row.

Jeremy was suddenly very hungry. Not taking his eyes off the rapidly crisping fish, he accepted a paper plate from his father and sat down, careful not to be next to Helene.

They had seven snappers apiece, and three were left over for Charlie. After the fish there were roasted potatoes and then big Long Island strawberries, winged with leaves for dipping in sugar. Jeremy stretched out on the beach and looked up at the sky. It was a brilliant blue overhead although a bank of white clouds, heavy and solid as day-old snowbanks, was moving in from the Connecticut shore.

The memory of the unpleasantness on the boat was still there, eating away at the edges of Jeremy's mind, but for the moment the sun was hot on his face and the air smelled sweet. He closed his eyes.

"Food maketh the man," the Professor said. Jeremy opened an eye to look at him.

"What does that mean, Uncle Bill?" Helene asked. Jeremy squeezed his eyes shut tight. He didn't have to look to know that Helene was giving his father that sweet-little-girl smile again.

"I'm not sure I have it right," the Professor said, "but I think it has something to do with everybody feeling better after a good meal."

Jeremy grinned and then sat up. "Listen, that was only breakfast," he said, "wait till you see me after lunch." He squinted up at the sky where the sun was almost at noon-day height. "Don't you think we ought to get going, Dad? Those fish won't be there all day."

"You're right. Start policing up, and we'll get started." He stood up and threw his paper plate into the fire. Jeremy stood up too.

"What does he mean about the fish? We already caught the fish," Helene said.

Jeremy looked down at her. Helene's arms were clutched tightly across her chest, as if she was cold.

"We have to finish the catch now," he said. "We always. . . ."

His father stopped him with a warning shake of his head. He leaned down toward Helene. "You look tired, honey," he said gently. "Would you rather go right home and not fish anymore today?"

Helene nodded.

"But, Dad!" Jeremy protested.

"Helene had a tiring day yesterday, and she was up very early," he told Jeremy firmly. "If she wants to go home, then home it is." He rested his hand on Jeremy's shoulder, but Jeremy shook it off.

He wouldn't look at his father as they finished cleaning up the campsite. Helene didn't bother to help, but sat huddled in a heap on the beach playing with the pebbles. Suddenly Jeremy heard her make a little sound of pleasure.

"Oh, what pretty shells!" she said. "What are these, Uncle Bill? I've never seen any like them before. There's a little hole in each one. If I had a lot I could string them together." Helene held her cupped hands to the Professor.

"Those are jingle shells," he said, smiling at her. "They're very special. Your mother and aunt used to make necklaces of them. There are lots of them on Pig Island, especially down at the other end just beyond that clump of pines." He pointed toward the jetty. Then he stooped over and pulled something out of the picnic basket. It was a large plastic bag with writing on it: *Honeywell Farms Bread.*

"Take this for the shells," he said. "Jeremy will show you where to find them."

Jeremy slammed down the skillet he was cleaning with sand. "No!" he cried. They both looked at him.

"I mean," he added, "those shells have to stay there." He knew he wasn't saying it right. His father's eyes hardened, but Jeremy couldn't stop. "She can't have them," he finished miserably.

There was silence. At last the Professor spoke. "You

go down to the jetty, Helene," he said. "I want to talk to Jeremy alone."

Jeremy shoved his hands deep into his pockets and stared defiantly after Helene as she started slowly down the beach. His lips tightened. Charlie was following her.

"I have tried to understand your motivation in behaving so badly toward your cousin," the Professor said slowly. "I do not discount sibling rivalry, of course. But it should not appear so soon—or so strongly. Helene has done nothing to you."

For a second Jeremy thought of telling his father what had happened on the boat. But what would be the use? He could hardly believe it himself. He stared stonily down at his feet and didn't answer.

"You may not like the situation Helene's coming has brought about, but that is no reason to resent her personally." The Professor stopped and appeared to be considering something. Jeremy began counting the holes in his sneakers.

"Listen, Jeremy." His father's voice was softer now. "The accident that took away your mother robbed Helene of both her parents. If I'd gone with them that day instead of my brother, *you'd* be the orphan now. Helene's been shuffled about from boarding school to hotels and back again since she was six years old. It *could* have been you."

Jeremy sighed and raised his head. His father smiled at him. "Try harder," he said. "Go on down to the jetty with Helene. Help her get some shells."

Jeremy nodded and started down the beach. Helene was out of sight now, somewhere behind the clump of pines.

48*

Passing the pines, he saw her sitting on the rocks near the jetty. A dark shape was near her on the sand: Charlie. Jeremy dragged his feet. What should he say to her? he wondered. Did she know what had happened to him that morning? And if so, could she make it happen again?

A few yards behind Helene, under the overhang of the low cliff, there was a patch of fog. Jeremy regarded it without interest at first, but as he came closer he realized that this particular piece of fog was behaving strangely. It was growing larger—and rapidly darkening. And then, just as the first icy finger of fear touched his neck, the fog reached out and enveloped his cousin completely.

Unreasoning panic seized Jeremy, but before he could force himself to move, the fog began to fade. In a moment he could see Helene again. She was standing up now, looking out over the water.

By the time Jeremy reached the jetty, there was no sign of the fog at all. Helene turned to him. She was smiling, and Jeremy regarded her warily.

"I came to help you get some shells," he said stiffly. He looked about for the plastic bag, but it wasn't there. "Where's the bag?" he asked.

Helene shrugged. "Shells?" she asked as if she'd never heard of them. "They're pretty, aren't they . . . but what would I do with them?"

Jeremy looked at her. Her mood seemed to have changed completely. Just see the way she was smiling, openly, without any of that shut-away look. "You don't want any shells now?" he asked cautiously.

Helene shook her head.

"Let's go then," he said hurriedly. He looked around. "Where's that dumb cat?" he wondered out loud. He called Charlie several times by name—but of course he never answered to his name anyhow. Feeling a little silly in front of Helene, Jeremy began singsonging Charlie's supper call: "Here kitty-kitty-kitty-kitty. . . ." Then he waited, expecting to hear a crash in the bushes as Charlie came hurtling toward him. But everything was quiet. As far as he could see the beach was empty.

"Just like him to run off when we're ready to leave," Jeremy said. Actually, it wasn't like Charlie at all. He usually stuck close when he was on the island, as if he never felt quite safe in the presence of so much water.

"He was right here with you, Helene. Didn't you see where he went?"

"He was here with me?"

Jeremy turned on her impatiently. "He was practically sitting on your feet a few minutes ago."

"Oh!" There was a flash of comprehension on Helene's face. Her hand flew to her mouth.

Jeremy's eyes narrowed and he took a step toward her. "What? . . ." he began and then stopped. There were nails on the fingers pressed to Helene's lips—long, strong fingernails. Jeremy shut his eyes for a second, then looked again. They were still there. Both hands were the same, fully equipped with fingernails.

5

"Your nails were bitten off!" Jeremy cried, pointing to Helene's hands. Last night playing cards, this morning in the boat, her fingers had ended in raw-looking little red stumps!

Helene's hand slowly came down from her face. For a long moment she stared at him, her eyes cold and hard with a knowledge he couldn't share.

"What *are* you anyway?" Jeremy whispered.

She smiled at him mechanically. "I'm Helene Wilson Hillis," she said. "My uncle is Professor William Hillis, and he lives on Quaker Path, Stony Point, Long Island, New York, United States of America. . . ." She stopped and looked around her. "The Earth," she finished.

"You're crazy," Jeremy said, backing away from her. One of them was, and the sooner he found out who, the better.

Helene held up her hands. "As for this"—she shrugged —"it happens to me all the time. They just grow. Fast." She looked him squarely in the eye.

"That's a lot of garbage," Jeremy said.

Helene sighed. "You don't believe me. It's *true*. I have a very rapid metabolism. My systolic rate is fantastic too," she added.

"It's still a lot of garbage." Jeremy's voice was firm, but he was wavering. What did systolic mean anyhow? He'd have to ask his father.

He cleared his throat. "Dad's waiting," he said. He'd put a few long strides between himself and Helene before he remembered Charlie. He stopped and called him once more.

"I'm sorry about him," she said. "But after all, it's only an animal."

Jeremy turned on her fiercely. "Only an animal! And what's that mangy Teddy of yours then? Some kind of a windup toy?" He stamped angrily off down the beach.

When they reached the campsite, they saw the Professor standing near the waterline with the neatly repacked picnic basket near his feet.

"Tide's turned," he told them. "Brought a wind with it. Looks as if it might be rough." He nodded toward the channel where whitecaps were frothing up at close intervals. The current in the shallows was stronger too, bumping the rowboat between the rocks.

"Did Charlie come back here?" Jeremy asked.

His father shook his head. "I thought he was with you."

"He was with Helene," Jeremy said, looking at her accusingly. She was staring out over the water toward the village, her hands in the folds of her sleeves. Jeremy wanted to draw his father's attention to them; then he remembered *systolic*. He'd better find out what that meant before he made a fool of himself.

"Come with me to look for Charlie, Dad?" he asked.

His father agreed and they went off, leaving Helene

sitting on the beach. As soon as they had climbed the low cliff leading onto the grassy plateau in the center of the island, Jeremy pulled his father to a stop.

"I want to ask you something. Don't ask me *why*, just tell me what you think." He hesitated, then plunged. "Could a person's fingernails ever grow a half an inch in, well, ten minutes or so?" Even as he said it, Jeremy knew the answer. When his father shook his head, he hastened to add, "I mean, if they had a fantastic, uh, systolic rate? Would that make a difference?"

The Professor laughed. "Someone's been pulling your leg, Jeremy, if they told you that. Half an inch of fingernail is about a two-month growth, I'd guess. What's it all about?"

Jeremy smiled with an angry satisfaction. "You'll see," he said.

They tramped back and forth across the narrow plateau, looking for Charlie. Finally the Professor called a halt.

"We've covered every inch of this section," he said. "Let's try something else. I'll go down and walk along the beach in one direction and you walk in the other. We'll meet at the jetty."

Jeremy set out for the end of the island once more, calling over and over for his cat. Once he heard a noise in the bushes above him, a businesslike scrabbling. He climbed quickly back onto the plateau. A blur of wings flashed up into his face and he stopped short. A marsh hen. He ran back down to the beach and walked on.

Nearing the jetty, he saw his father several hundred yards away on the other side. He waved at Jeremy at the same time that he shook his head. Jeremy thought he was beginning to look worried.

At the jetty they met and then stood looking out at the water. The incoming tide lashed the waves against the rocks.

"Maybe he has a mole, or a bird, cornered somewhere and doesn't want to leave it," the Professor suggested.

Jeremy shook his head. Charlie wasn't that ambitious a hunter.

"Where did you see him last?"

"Right here." Jeremy stepped up to the shoreline where the breakwater began. "He was sitting here, next to Helene."

His father came up and put his arm around Jeremy's shoulders. "Could he have walked out there, do you think?" He pointed to the narrow shelf of the breakwater extending into the roughening Sound. Jeremy looked too until comprehension came to him.

"Aw, no!" he cried. "He wouldn't do a dumb thing like that." He felt the heat rush to his face and turned angrily on his father. "He wouldn't do that!"

"You have to consider it, Jeremy," his father told him quietly. "Maybe you just didn't see him run out there."

"There was this funny fog," Jeremy began, and then his voice got stuck in his throat. It *could* have happened, just the way his father said. The Professor's arm tightened around Jeremy's shoulders, and he let himself be led back to the campsite like a little boy.

Helene was sitting next to the picnic basket where they had left her. Head bent over, one hand at her mouth, she didn't look up until they were next to her. Then she stood up. "Are we going now?" she asked.

She began buttoning her sweater, and now Jeremy saw that the nails were short, the flesh above them red and raw. He shook his head, sank suddenly to the sand, and leaned his forehead on his knees. The whole day had been crazy, and in the middle of all the craziness Charlie had disappeared.

"Do you want to try calling Charlie some more?" Jeremy's father asked gently. "We can wait a bit longer— although the wind is getting strong." He squinted up at the sky where grayish clouds were rapidly replacing the open stretches of blue.

Jeremy shook his head wordlessly. If Charlie had been able to come he would have by now. He stood up and walked over to the pine tree where he'd snagged the anchor, and released it. Then he stepped into the shallows where the boat was.

"If he's on the island hiding or sleeping, he'll be safe," his father said as they started rowing toward the harbor. It wasn't a very convincing argument, but Jeremy clung to it.

The waves in the channel were rough; soon it was all they could do to keep the little boat on course. The prow slapped into each whitecap, sending a shower of spray over them all. Once, after a particularly heavy drenching, Jeremy turned around to see how Charlie was managing. The seat in the prow was empty. He bent his head low over the oars so that Helene couldn't see his face.

Entering the harbor, they were suddenly surrounded by

other boats: sailboats tacking in on sharp diagonals, motor launches swishing arrogantly past to add big bumpy swells to their rowing problems. The ominous sky and gusty wind were sending everyone home in a hurry.

"Looks like a good blow," Jeremy heard a familiar voice announce as they swung in next to the float at the end of the dock. Glancing up, he saw Captain Harry looking down at them.

Captain Harry Dachenhausen, Magda's husband, was a big man. Viewed from below, he assumed grotesque proportions. Only the tip of his Navy cap and a small sticking-out wedge of red beard could be seen above the vast barrel of his belly.

"You!" Jeremy heard Helene cry. He turned around to see her staring wide-eyed at the Captain.

"Well, sure." The big man raised an eyebrow as he sent a puzzled look above her head to Jeremy's father.

Helene looked confused and quickly bent to gather up some of the fishing gear from the floor of the boat. By the time his father was through making the usual introductions, Jeremy could see that she was once more in control of herself. Whatever had caused her surprise at seeing Captain Harry was gone, and she was able to acknowledge his presence with a polite smile and a murmured "How-do-you-do?" Had she heard about Captain Harry from Magda? It was possible, but Jeremy was too tired to worry about it all just then—there were so many strange things about his cousin. As he picked up his gear and threw it onto the float all he could think of was how Charlie was always the first one out of the boat.

"Better get her up onto the float, Bill," the Captain advised Jeremy's father. "This is going to be a good one." Grabbing the top rung of the ladder, he swung himself down onto the float. It rocked violently for a second, steadying itself only when the Captain spread his treelike legs to apply a little counterbalance.

Now, with the Captain at one end and Jeremy and his father at the other, they swung the rowboat up onto the float. Iron rungs in the dock pilings supplied a stationary mooring, and in a few minutes ropes from prow and stern fastened the little boat securely to the dock.

"There," said the Captain, giving a final yank to his clove hitch, "that ought to do it." He turned to Jeremy. "What's the matter with you, skipper? You look as if you lost your best friend!"

Of course the Captain didn't know what he was saying, but it was too much for Jeremy. Shaking the Captain's hamlike hand from his arm, he ran over to the ladder and began scrambling up it. At the top he paused and looked down.

"Need any more help, Dad?" he asked in a strangled sort of voice that he hardly recognized as his own. "Because if you don't, I'd like to go home."

"Just take your pole," his father said, handing it up to him. He held onto the end of it for a moment as Jeremy took it.

"Don't give up hope," he told him softly. Jeremy nodded, then turned quickly and started running across the parking lot toward the village.

In the shopping area on Main Street some of the storekeepers were standing out on the sidewalk looking toward the harbor. The flower baskets hanging from the lampposts were beginning to swing in the wind, and little Mrs. Reid from the Goodie Shoppe was wandering up and down worrying about them to anyone who would listen. Normally she was one of Jeremy's favorite people, but today he passed her by without a word and went on up the hill toward Quaker Path. All he wanted to do was to get home and lock himself in his room.

He made it all the rest of the way home without meeting anyone. Slipping into the house by the kitchen door, he stopped when he heard Magda's steps in the living room. When he heard the front screen door slam and knew she had gone out onto the porch, he ran up the stairs to his room.

Here he locked the door and flung himself down on the bed, where he lay staring up at the ceiling. The whole day had been wrong from the start, beginning with Helene's appearance in the kitchen. Jeremy shifted about restlessly. Trying to figure out Helene was like trying to unwrap a ball of cobwebs. Anyhow, it didn't really matter about her. Charlie was gone.

Had there really been time for the cat to run out onto the breakwater when the fog came up? And if Charlie had fallen in, wouldn't Jeremy have noticed something? He flung his arms above his head as he thought of the answer to that. Charlie could have fallen down on the far side of the breakwater where the waves were so turbulent that his struggles would not have been apparent to anyone. The undertow was bad there too, sucking away at the jagged rocks with persistent strength. Jeremy turned over and buried his face in the pillow.

A dull pounding woke him. He sat up and, seeing the darkness of his room, wondered how long he had slept. It wasn't until there was a flash of lightning and a clap of thunder that he realized it wasn't nighttime. The storm had come. The pounding was his window shutter banging against the wall of the house. He stumbled across the room and, leaning out of the window, reached for the shutter. He'd no sooner touched it than the sky seemed to open up with a torrent of rain. It came crashing down onto the lawn and street below, making the bushes along the path bow to the ground. By the time Jeremy had fastened down the shutter his head and arms were soaking wet.

How Charlie hated storms. He usually waited them out in Jeremy's clothes closet or in the back of the woodbox downstairs, depending on which part of the house Jeremy was in at the time. Jeremy could imagine him now out on the island, trying to find shelter beneath one of the scraggly pines. Or was he crying up and down the shore-line looking for the boat?

We left too soon! Jeremy thought in a panic. We should have waited, looked more.

Well, he knew what he had to do. Softly opening his door, he slipped out into the hall. Helene's room was dark although a flap of wings as he went past told him it wasn't empty.

When Jeremy was on the stairs, he heard voices coming from the living room. Magda, Helene, and his father were in there. He tiptoed down, avoiding the creaky steps, and then, holding his breath, crept past the archway to the living room. The front door swung open as smooth as silk. Outside, the wind and the rain roared about him, covering the sound of his footsteps as he ran down the flagstone path toward the road.

No cars, no people were to be seen anywhere. As Jeremy ran down the center of the road toward the village, the big maples on either side of him turned inside out like old umbrellas as the wind whipped at them. The stores on Main Street were closed up, some of the front windows barricaded with iron gratings. And someone, Mrs. Reid probably, had taken down the baskets of flowers from the streetlights.

In the harbor there were still a few men tying their boats up on the shore, but out on the water a state of siege already existed as the surging waves tried to tear the battened-down boats from their moorings. Jeremy ran out to the end of the dock and let himself down the ladder to the float. Waves were breaking over it; he had to drop to his hands and knees to reach the boat. Soaking wet, Captain Harry's clove hitches were twice as hard to undo. Jeremy pulled and tugged until his fingers felt raw. At last he untied the knot at the prow. One end of the boat swung free.

"Jeremy!" A high-pitched cry cut through the drumming rain. Jeremy looked up to see Helene leaning over the edge of the dock. Water was streaming down her face and dripping off the ends of her hair.

"Go home!" he shouted.

Helene shook her head. "You mustn't go," she told him,

her eyes looking desperate. "You'll be killed out in this storm!"

The thought had already crossed Jeremy's mind, but he had decided to ignore it.

"Go home," he repeated.

Helene swished the wet hair out of her eyes with one hand and leaned farther out over the edge of the dock.

"Listen, Jeremy," she said rapidly. "Your cat isn't out on the island. Don't bother looking for him."

Jeremy gave her a glance of disgust and turned back to the rope. One more loop and he would have it. He gritted his teeth and pulled, but Captain Harry's knot held.

"Jeremy!" Helene's voice wailed in tune with the rising wind. "You can't go. No one must get hurt. They promised me no one would get hurt!" From the uneven spacing of her words, Jeremy guessed that she was beginning to cry. He didn't look up.

"Get out of here!" he yelled as he gave a violent tug at the knot.

Helene didn't answer, but suddenly he felt the float lurch. Whirling about, he saw her standing behind him. She was swaying back and forth and holding onto the side of the boat. Leaning forward, she thrust her face close to his.

"Stupid, stupid!" she screamed at him. "Don't you see? I'm not Helene!"

She shook her head wildly, and Jeremy felt the ends of her hair whip his cheeks. She's crazy, really crazy, he thought as he backed away from her.

"I'm not Helene," she cried again, coming closer.

61*

"Helene is gone, gone to Terra. *And your cat's gone with her.*"

Just then the knot pulled out and the rowboat swung loose. Helene stumbled and clutched at Jeremy's arm.

He felt the touch no more than a firecracker would feel the match. The ensuing explosion blotted out everything. It was around him and inside him at the same time. There was no escaping it, no use trying to hang on. He felt himself dissolving, breaking up into whirling bits of dark and light. Consciousness left him.

When he was himself again, he was treading water in bright sunlight. Ahead of him, the familiar islands of the Sound lay on a glassy expanse of blue. He could see the rocky breakwater of Pig Island jutting out in the channel.

But where was the storm? Slowly he turned around until he faced the harbor. It was crowded with boats, ten times as many as had been there before. And, despite the bright sunlight, some of them lay in shadow, for at the shoreline, east of the village, a massive gray building, tall as a skyscraper, reached up to blot out the sun.

6

Jeremy treaded water automatically while his mind strug-
gled to take in the scene before him. His heart began to
pound. Combined with the pressure of the water, it soon
made him feel as if he were suffocating. He turned
slowly to look at the Sound again. That *was* Pig Island out
there. To the right of it lay the western arm of the harbor
where the lighthouse was; to the left, the bulky shape of
Old Fort crowned the tip of the eastern curve. Beyond
everything were the familiar low curves of the Connecticut
shoreline.

I'm going to drown, he thought, drawing in a great
sobbing breath.

His arms and legs continued to work, however, and
gradually, as one sobbing breath followed another, his
heartbeat slowed. He started to swim toward the shore,
keeping his eyes fixed on the patch of water immediately
ahead of him, and avoiding the sight of the strange tall
building. With a tiny corner of his mind he noticed that
he was using the energy-saving sidestroke his father had
taught him for emergencies. He could not, therefore, be
completely crazy.

The alternative to being crazy was to be dreaming. Yet
he was real, the water was real. . . . He couldn't remem-

ber how he had got into it in the first place, but that was the way dreams were.

As he swam toward the harbor Jeremy was impressed again by the number of boats. How had they all got there so fast? Surely it was only a few minutes ago that he had stood on the float arguing with Helene.

But where were all the usual boats? These craft were different from the white-painted cruisers and bright sailboats customarily dotting Stony Point harbor. These boats were worn and weathered to dull grays and browns. No paint showed anywhere on them; nor were there any nameplates, just lines of black caulking messily striping the sides. A strong fishy smell blew from them as Jeremy came closer.

Now he could see string nets spread out over the decks of many of the boats. Although there were no signs of life on any of them, they were all moored with neatly furled sails and gave the impression of being well used. Above all, it was the ordinariness of the scene that struck terror into Jeremy. *When had all these boats arrived?* Without wanting to, his eyes sought out the tall building on the shore, and he felt strength drain out of him. He squeezed his eyes shut—and a moment later felt a hard blow on his right temple. He opened his eyes. A chunky piece of driftwood was bobbing about in front of his face. Raising his hand with an effort, he pushed it away.

A red mist was seeping into his right eye. Looking down, Jeremy saw the water turning pink below his neck. As the throbbing pain in his temple increased, he knew it was too far to shore and too far to reach for a handhold on one of the boats' anchor lines.

He let his arms and legs sag down into the water until he was limply suspended with just his nose surfacing. It was the survival position his father had taught him. If he could just stay relaxed and sustain it, maybe he could rest for a while and then swim to shore. But even as he reasoned things out, Jeremy felt his muscles tense up and his body begin to sink. He gasped for breath and took in a mouthful of salt water. Panic took over. His arms and legs thrashed wildly about.

Help me! he thought. Someone help me!

Then, just as he was about to go under for a second time, he heard a familiar voice. *"Don't let go. Hang on. I'm coming."*

He didn't stop to think that with the water in his ears and the sound of his struggling breath filling his head, he couldn't really be hearing Captain Harry talk to him. All Jeremy knew was that the voice was there. And it gave him strength. Looking toward the shore, he saw a large red-headed figure waving to him from the dock. Blinking and gasping for breath, he watched as Captain Harry rapidly swung down into a rowboat. Powerful pulls sent the boat skimming toward him.

"Hang on, boy." This time the voice was more solid and definitely came from the man in the boat. Soon Jeremy could make out the anxious face above the oars. Captain Harry's blue eyes smiled encouragement at him, and Jeremy kept his head above water as he came nearer. Then he was there, and Jeremy was hauled up over the side of the boat.

"Over the seat. Keep your head down. That's it," the

65*

familiar voice told him. Jeremy lay with his face on the sun-warmed seat as a heavy hand pounded on his back.

"OK, OK," he gasped at last, pulling himself partway up onto the seat. The red-bearded man surveyed him anxiously.

"All right now, boy?" he asked. When Jeremy nodded, he settled himself back at the oars. "Then we'd best head for shore. All the boats have been in for an hour. Which boat are you off, anyhow?"

Captain Harry wasn't making much sense, thought Jeremy groggily. "Boat? Why, my own, I guess," he answered slowly, remembering a little something now. "I was on the dock in a storm. I was sort of knocked out, I think." Jeremy shoved the wet hair back out of his eyes. "What's happened, Captain Harry?" he asked.

The big man snorted. "Thanks for the promotion." He smiled over his shoulder at Jeremy before beginning to row.

"You know," he continued, "that's not much of a story to account for being out after hours. There's been no storm today." Pulling hard on the oars, he headed the boat toward shore.

Maybe Jeremy had been in the water longer than he thought. Maybe, he decided, he'd been unconscious for days and everything had changed.

"Is it still Friday?" he asked cautiously.

The man laughed. "All day," he answered.

"June twenty-second?"

"Uh huh. Say!" The big man twisted around to look at Jeremy. "You've had a bad knock on the head." He pulled a cloth from his pocket. "Press this to it for a while and don't try to talk anymore."

Jeremy took the handkerchief and pressed it to his temple. It came away bloodied, and he let his head fall to his knees. He heard the Captain murmur something in a sympathetic tone, but he didn't answer. Friday. Still Friday. What had happened? He kept his head down as Captain Harry continued to row steadily toward the shore. He didn't look up until he heard a voice hailing them.

Directly ahead was the pier, and near the end of it was a group of men. One of them was waving at the rowboat. All the men were bearded, and they were dressed alike in shapeless brown overalls. Jeremy had never seen any of them before.

"Captain Harry," he cried. "Who are they?"

The big man didn't answer right away, but with a powerful tug sent the little boat up against the pier. As it bumped against the pilings, he raised the oars to a resting position.

"Now then," he said. "Maybe it's about time I asked some of the questions. I think you'd better tell me what really happened." The Captain's voice was serious. "To begin with, that's the second time you've called me Captain. I'm Harry all right, but never Captain. Are you trying to keep from telling me the name of your boat?"

"What are you talking about?" cried Jeremy. "Captain Harry, you act as if you don't even know me!"

The big man smiled apologetically. "There are so many boys training here this summer. . . . I can't say that I place you right off."

Jeremy ran his tongue over suddenly dry lips.

"Don't joke, Captain Harry! Please," he whispered.

The red-bearded man had only time to give Jeremy a puzzled stare before one of the men above tossed down a rope. Harry caught it and clipped the boat in against the pilings. Standing up, he steadied the boat with his legs and motioned toward the ladder in the side of the dock.

"Up you go, boy," he said to Jeremy, "while I hold her still." Jeremy looked up into the strange faces. The men had a wild appearance, but strangely enough, his fear of them vanished. Little bits of sympathetic thought seemed to curl out from them, enclosing him in a feeling of good-will. He didn't stop to wonder how he knew that, but started willingly toward the reaching hands.

Harry was right behind him. "He got a blow on the head," he said, putting an arm about Jeremy's shoulders. "He's a bit dazed." The men crowded around them.

"Whose boat is he off?" This was one of the younger men, scarcely more than a boy, with his half inch of golden beard catching the sunlight.

Harry shrugged. "Hasn't said," he answered.

The younger man grinned at Jeremy. "Maybe he'd rather not say. But don't worry so, man; they can't kill you!"

Jeremy looked from one strange bearded face to another. They were so friendly, so peaceful, and like the boats, their ordinariness terrified him. He tightened his lips and shook his head. Immediately the men moved closer, and the comforting feelings coming from them grew stronger.

"Say," young blond beard exclaimed excitedly, "take a

look at his clothes. No yeoman ever owned those! Maybe he fell off one of the ocean-fleet vessels!"

"Are you from Stony Point, boy?" Harry asked gently.

Jeremy nodded. At least he was sure of *that*.

"But his clothes . . ." began the young man.

Harry shook his head warningly. "I feel that he speaks the truth," he said firmly. The younger man was silent. "And yet. . . ." Harry frowned. "There is something wrong here."

"Everything is wrong," Jeremy burst out. "Captain Harry, why are you pretending not to know me?"

Harry sighed. "Listen, boy," he said slowly. "I have never seen you before in my life. Can't you tell that that is true speaking?"

Suddenly Jeremy could. Looking into the kind blue eyes of the man before him he knew that he was a stranger—no matter how much he might look like his own Captain Harry. With the loss of his friend went Jeremy's only hope of making any sense. He *was* in a dream then. He shook the arm off his shoulder. "I'm all right," he said stiffly.

"Then perhaps you will tell us from whose boat you come," a white-bearded man suggested politely. "Then we could take you to him, and you could, ah, make whatever explanations you wish."

"I live on Quaker Path," Jeremy said.

The men exchanged amused glances.

"You are a yeoman then," the blond boy said, sounding a bit disappointed.

None of this conversation made any sense to Jeremy,

69*

but he didn't care now. After all, in a dream anything could happen. He allowed the men to lead him down the dock toward the village.

It was the same and yet not the same, with just the grotesque changes that one might expect in a dream. The parking lot was there, just beyond the dock, but there were only two cars in it and they were so old that they should have been in a museum. The square was where it should have been too, but it was crowded with strangers, most of them bearded men in faded brown overalls. And there was the Hercules monument, only today the paint was washed away and the wood showed through, cracked and brown.

They passed through the crowd quickly. For the most part the strangers around him seemed unusually affable to Jeremy, greeting each other with quiet smiles and nods of pleased recognition. When they reached Main Street, Jeremy looked about him with a detached interest that was based entirely on his determination to consider himself in a dream. There were the stores right where they were supposed to be, although they were smaller and darker and much dirtier than they were in real life. Business seemed to be good anyhow; an endless stream of women with shopping baskets passed in and out of the banging screen doors.

The streetlamps were exactly the same—except that there were no baskets of flowers hanging from them. As they went around the corner from Main to Parker Street, Jeremy was tempted to reach out and clasp one of the lampposts, it looked so solid and real somehow. But just as he was about to touch it he pulled back his hand. Suppose it *was* real, then what? He shook his head, and the movement made him utter a small sigh of pain.

"Head still hurt?" the blond boy asked him.

Jeremy smiled weakly. "It's all right," he said.

On Parker Street the buildings seemed to be dwellings, to judge from the lines of wash near them. But they were very small houses, looking much like the summer cottages along the beach at home. Backyards seemed nonexistent; one house was built right next to the other, with hardly arm room between.

Jeremy doggedly hung onto his detachment. "Stony Point certainly has grown, hasn't it?" he said conversationally.

The blond boy gave him a startled look and then laughed. "You're a cool one, aren't you?" he said. "A few minutes ago you were too scared to say what ship you were off and now you can make a joke."

At the end of Parker Street they stopped. There were no street signs here, nothing but a wide iron gate stretching across the road. Beyond the gate was a group of large wooden buildings.

"Which barrack is yours?" Harry turned around to look at Jeremy.

"Barrack?" Jeremy stared at him.

The blond boy laughed again. "Sure, barrack," he said. "This is Quaker Path. There's nothing but barracks from here on over to the highway."

"But I don't live *here*." Jeremy felt his detachment begin to slip. He shivered suddenly and the little group closed in on him once more. The old man murmured something about a doctor, and he turned on him angrily.

"I'm not sick," he cried. "Listen to me. All of you, listen to me." He grabbed the blond boy's arm. The flesh was warm and solid beneath the jersey—too real for a dream. "I *did* live here. I mean, I do live on Quaker Path but . . . I've always lived on Quaker Path. My father and I have always lived on Quaker Path. . . ." Jeremy knew he was babbling, but he couldn't stop.

"Slowly, boy, slowly," Harry said. "Is your father here in Stony Point?"

"Yes, yes!" Jeremy cried. "He's at the University."

"The University!" The blond boy freed himself from Jeremy's grasp and stepped back.

"Are you one of the . . . students?" Harry asked gently.

"No, of course not," Jeremy answered impatiently. "But my father works there. He's Professor Hillis."

"Hillis!" Several of the men in the crowd repeated the name, and for a moment it hung in the air like a sigh. Then, like the blond boy, the men pulled away, and the warm feeling of friendship Jeremy had felt disappeared.

"You're Hillis's son," Harry said. His voice was sad.

Jeremy began to shiver again, but this time no silent thoughts of comfort came to him. One by one the group dispersed, moving quietly off down the street toward the village. In a moment there was no one with him except Harry. He was looking beyond Jeremy toward the harbor. Jeremy looked that way too.

"The University," Harry said. His voice had an angry sound.

72*

East of the village, on the shore, the great gray monolith Jeremy had seen from the water rose up to dwarf the buildings around it. There were no windows or ornamentation of any kind on its smooth gray walls.

"That's the University?" Jeremy whispered.

"You know it is," Harry said wearily. "But something has happened to your head. Perhaps. . . ." He looked thoughtful. "Perhaps you are not clear about anything and your father is not Hillis?"

That was one thing Jeremy was certain of. He shook his head, ignoring the little shocks of pain it gave him. "My father is William Hillis," he said firmly.

Harry sighed. "Then I will take you to him. But first, I think you should rest a bit, put some ice on your head. My house is just down the street. We'll go there."

Harry was silent as they walked down the street together. What had happened to the friendliness and sympathy he'd radiated earlier? For Jeremy the whole experience had rapidly gone from dream to nightmare and now, worst of all, it seemed to be turning into reality.

Harry's house was just like the other little houses that lined the streets row after row. Inside, its meager furnishings bore out the summer-cottage idea to Jeremy: one easy chair, a plain wooden table, a stove up on legs, a tin sink and, over near the door, a tall brown box that Jeremy didn't recognize at all. He sat at the table and watched as Harry went to the box and opened it to reveal a large chunk of ice inside. He chipped at it with a pointed instrument until he'd gathered together a handful, which he wrapped in a clean towel.

An icebox . . . and the old-fashioned cars. . . .

"Harry! What . . . what. . . ?" Jeremy stuttered in his excitement. "What year. . . ?" Then he stopped as his eyes fell on a calendar on the wall above the sink. The year was the same. So much for that theory. Jeremy rested his elbows on the table and buried his face in his hands.

"Try this, it will make you feel better." He looked up to see Harry standing above him with the ice. He let him press it to his head and then obediently held it there himself.

"Now," said Harry, sitting down in the chair opposite, "what did you want to ask me?"

"Nothing," Jeremy said dully. "Nothing at all."

"Well then, let me talk a bit. Perhaps if we go over what happened, your mind will become clearer. First of all, you must have fallen off a boat since you had all your clothes on when you were out there getting yourself drowned. You *were* drowning, you know. If I hadn't been there to catch your sending, you would have."

Jeremy was following along fairly well until this strange word appeared.

"My 'sending,'" he said. "What's that?"

"It was a clear sending," Harry said, looking surprised. "Of course, it always is when there's fear."

"But . . . a 'sending' . . . what's that?" Jeremy asked again.

"A two-year-old knows what a sending is," Harry said. "The blow on your head must be worse than I thought. Does it pain you much?"

Jeremy slammed the ice pack down on the table. "Never mind my head," he shouted. "Why doesn't anybody believe me when I say I don't know? I don't know anything: what this place is, who you are, *anything!*"

The desperation in his voice must have got through to Harry. For a moment he looked at Jeremy with a piercingly direct gaze, which Jeremy bore without flinching.

"I believe you," he said at last. "At least, I believe you when you say you don't know." Then Harry nodded to himself as if he'd come to some decision. "Do I have your permission?" he asked.

"My what?" Jeremy asked.

"Your permission. I am a Prober and, of course, I must have your permission to enter your mind." Harry spoke slowly and carefully.

He still thinks I was knocked crazy by that piece of driftwood, Jeremy thought. He said, "Sure, you have my permission. Go ahead."

"Look at me then," Harry directed. Jeremy did, and felt a little click somewhere behind his eyes. He knew he couldn't look away if he tried; his eyes were locked to Harry's with a strong invisible bond.

"Think of your home," Harry directed. "And your father."

Jeremy thought about Quaker Path, the way it really was, with the big maples making a shady tunnel all the way up. He thought of the white colonial house and the yard full of flowering lavender and forsythia. He imagined that the front door was opening and his father was coming out. Suddenly it was all too much for him and he let the picture fade away.

"Like that," he whispered.

Harry brushed his hand across his eyes and broke the contact. There was an incredulous look on his face. "Unless I've lost my power," he said slowly, "that was true thinking, and that *was* Hillis—I've seen him. But my boy, there is no place like that in Stony Point. Not in all Terra, as far as I know."

Terra. Jeremy's mind whirled. Suddenly he was back on the dock in the storm. A white-faced girl was screaming at him, her voice cutting through the drumming rain. "I'm not Helene. Helene is gone—gone to Terra. And your cat's gone with her." She had touched him before he. . . .

Jeremy grabbed Harry's arm. "Terra!" he shouted. "What is Terra?"

"The world is Terra," the big man said, looking at him with eyes filled with pity. "You have forgotten *much!*" He stood up. "We must get you to your father—that much is true. I'm sure he will try to help you."

"No, wait." Jeremy jumped up. "I live on Earth. Isn't this Earth?" He clutched at Harry's arm.

"This is Stony Point, Long Island, United States of America, Terra," Harry told him carefully. "Earth?" He frowned. *"Earth?* I've never heard of such a place."

7 ✷

For a long moment the man and the boy stared at each other. Harry was the first to speak.

"Could it be another planet?" He frowned. "But that couldn't be it. You know this town . . . and you claim that man Hillis as your father." He looked quite stunned.

Jeremy was too busy trying to sort things out in his own head to notice the slurring emphasis Harry gave to the name Hillis.

"That's what makes it so awful," he said dully. "It's so close to being home . . . but it's not." His throat grew tight and he sat down heavily on the kitchen chair again. After a second he looked up. "Could you do it again?" he asked. "Look into my mind, I mean. Maybe you can figure out how I got here."

Jeremy had been conscious of nothing more than the eye connection and a little tickle somewhere in the back of his head while Harry had looked into his mind. Apparently it was harder on Harry than on him. The big man looked tired, older in some indefinable way, almost as if some of his life had been drained from him.

"I can't," Harry said, running a hand over his eyes. "I can't do it again—not right away."

"Then let me tell you what I remember," Jeremy said

slowly. "Maybe then you won't go on thinking I've been knocked crazy or something."

"Maybe." Harry smiled thinly.

Jeremy began to describe his experience on the dock in the storm, but even as he spoke, he realized that he would have to go back farther than that. Excitement rose in him as some of the pieces began to fit together. If what the girl on the dock—and who was she?—had told him was true, then Helene and Charlie had "gone to Terra" earlier in the day. They had gone when the swirling mist enveloped them both on the island!

Now the words came tumbling out of Jeremy. "That wasn't Helene on the beach! I *knew* she couldn't grow fingernails that fast. But when we came back after looking for Charlie. . . . She must have chewed them all off!" If he hadn't been so upset about Charlie he would have looked more closely at her hands. Then he thought of something else. "But that means—that means they're both on Terra! Helene and Charlie. And my father, he might be here too."

"This whirling mist you speak of. . . . There is something the Probers talk about secretly that sounds much like that. But how could it be?" Harry looked at Jeremy speculatively. "You know this town—granted it is different." He raised his hand as Jeremy started to interrupt him. "And since the man you saw in your mind as your father looks very much like Hillis—what little I have seen of him—I guess there is only one thing to do and that is to take you to him. But I would rather not."

"Why? Why don't you want to take me to him?"

The big man looked unhappy. "There is something wrong at the University. The people there, even the ones we have known for years, are not open to our feelings anymore. They are closed off, as if they were hiding something."

"My father wouldn't be mixed up in anything wrong," Jeremy said stiffly.

"Your father. . . ." Harry sighed. "What about that house of his?"

"House! But it wasn't there. Our house wasn't on Quaker Path," Jeremy told him.

"Of course not. The Hillis stronghold is out on the east arm of the harbor, in a stone fortress built in the days of the Last Great War."

"Old Fort!" Jeremy interrupted.

"You know it?" Harry didn't wait for his answer. "But of course, if he is your father. . . . It is strange how your mind has been twisted."

This time Jeremy was quiet. What was the use in denying it. *He* knew he was all right even if no one else did.

"Go on about the house," he said. "What's wrong with it?"

"There are gates and strong walls to keep people away from the fort, but those who have gotten close say there are men there with guns. We have not needed guns for a hundred years. What is he hiding? Surely more than the scientific miracles we've heard about: the trains that run without steam, the lights that glow without kerosene. There must be something else, something not good." Abruptly he stood up. "But there is nothing else to do.

He is your father. I'll take you over to the University."

They went back to the village the same way they had come, Jeremy staying close to Harry's side as they passed through the crowded square. The strange thing was that here and there he saw someone who made him stop and look again. The people of this Stony Point were poorly dressed—the women wore none of the brightly colored summer dresses that Jeremy was used to, and the men and boys were uniformly clothed in brown overalls—and yet, here and there, he saw a face that looked familiar. A second glance, however, always proved him wrong. That was not really Peter Stein or David Olson. The woman in the doorway to the candy store was not really Mrs. Reid—although until he was within three feet of her he wasn't sure.

He grew more and more confused as they went on. The fact that these people seemed happier and more relaxed than the people in his town made no difference. By the time they reached the road leading to the University, he was feeling too depressed to respond to Harry's attempts at conversation.

"Soon you'll see your father and he will straighten you out," Harry said. Then he came to a sudden stop. They were at the entrance to the University. "This is as far as I go," he added. "You're sure now, very sure, that your father is Dr. Hillis?"

"Professor," Jeremy said automatically. "He doesn't have his Ph.D. yet. Yes, I'm sure." It was the one thing he was sure of.

"Then you must go in here," Harry told him. Still he made no move to go. "I must leave you now. I have my

80*

job to do." He looked toward the dock. "See, there are the new yeomen waiting for me. Twice a day at low tide we go out to tend to the oyster beds."

Jeremy looked and saw twenty or thirty boys in brown standing near the end of the dock. *Yeomen.* Just something else that didn't make sense.

"I must go," Harry repeated. Two steps, and he turned around again. "You know where I live," he said.

Jeremy nodded, then straightened his shoulders. "I'll be all right," he said. "And thanks."

A final clap on the shoulder, and Harry was striding back along the road. Jeremy watched him until his red head and broad shoulders were swallowed up by the crowd of boys. Then he turned his face toward the University.

The entrance was a narrow opening cut into the gray stone slab of the wall. The instant he stepped within it Jeremy felt the chill of stone close about him, and he ran quickly toward a door at the end of the passage. In the top section of the door was a tiny square of dark glass that shone with a dull light. But nowhere was there a bell or a knocker. Jeremy rapped on the wood of the door. Then he waited. After about half a minute he thought he saw something move behind the glass. He knocked again, and waited some more. At last the door swung open.

In the half light he could see the pale oval of a face above a shapeless dark mass. He felt someone take his arm firmly. A few steps in the darkness, and then another door swung open and he stepped into sunlight.

Or at least it seemed like sunlight. It took him a few seconds to realize that the large modern room he was in had no windows. The apparent sunlight had to come from concealed lighting of some sort. It reminded him of a doctor's office in the interior of a building. Shiny green plants massed in the corners and a large lighted fish tank completed the illusion.

His guide flung the dark cloak from her shoulders and turned to him. She was a young girl, possibly twenty years old, dressed in a military-looking green dress. She followed Jeremy's gaze toward the aquarium.

"Fish are not legally pets, you know," she said stiffly. Then she went to the other side of a large desk in a corner of the room and pulled a notebook out of the drawer.

"All right," she began briskly. "When did you L.W.O.C.?"

"Huh?" Jeremy stared at her.

"Leave without consent," the girl explained impatiently. "You're one of Dr. Robertson's students, there's no use denying it. You were a smart boy to know that you had to come back—although," she said, looking at him suspiciously, "you seem fully rehabilitated to me. Suppose we start at the beginning. Give me your name and room number." She bent over the notebook expectantly.

"I . . . I . . . ." Jeremy started stuttering. Then he stopped and took a deep breath. There was no reason why he should feel guilty about not having a room number!

"I'm Jeremy Hillis," he said firmly. "I don't have a room number, and I want to see my father."

The point of the young woman's pencil snapped. Her head came up.

"Hillis? You say your name is Hillis?"

"Yes. My father is Doctor—I mean, Professor Hillis."

The young woman stood up. Eyeing Jeremy warily, she took a few steps backward until her face was next to a small grilled opening in the wall. She slid her fingers along the front of the grill, touching a series of small buttons. A harsh buzzing came from the grill. When it stopped she spoke.

"Reception desk, main entrance," she said, not taking her eyes off Jeremy. "I have here a boy who claims to be Dr. Hillis's son. It may be a negative reaction. Code Red."

A tinny voice inquired about Jeremy's room number. He frowned at the girl.

"No knowledge. He is damaged. Repeat: Code Red." Her voice took on an urgency, and Jeremy exploded.

"I'm not a negative . . . whatever," he shouted. "And I'm not damaged! I want to see my father!"

It was bad enough having the friendly men in the village turn away from him in fear when he'd announced his name. Now this snippy female was trying to get him arrested or something.

"Code Red. Code Red," the girl began babbling into the grill, a look of real fear on her face.

Jeremy decided to take another approach.

"Look, miss," he began, trying to keep his voice down, "I'm not dangerous or anything. I just want to get a few things straightened out."

The girl made a visible effort to control her breathing, swallowed twice, then spoke again. "That's right. You will be straightened out." She smiled mechanically at Jeremy. "The doctors will help you. Can you say that with me? Let's try it. The-doctors-will-help-me . . . the-doctors-will-help-me. . . ."

"Stop it!" Jeremy banged his hand down on the desk, making the notebook jump. The girl tried to press herself into the wall.

"Code Red! Code Red!" she cried. Suddenly Jeremy saw her eyes flick to something behind him. He whirled around just in time to see a door slide open in the rear wall. Two burly men in green uniforms stepped into the room. Walking quickly and in step, they came up on either side of Jeremy.

"Come along, young fellow," said the taller of the two men. His voice was not unkind. Jeremy felt hands on his arms, but he was determined to try once more the statement that seemed to get him into so much trouble and yet was all he had to cling to.

"I'm Jeremy Hillis," he said, keeping his arms glued firmly to his sides. "And I want to see my father."

"You see?" said the girl. "Damaged. He's really damaged."

"That's a new approach, though," said the man on Jeremy's left, looking up at the taller man with a wink. "Usually they can't say anything, and this one even lies!"

"I'm not lying!"

Jeremy's shout made the men tighten their grip on his arms. "Easy, young fellow," said the tall man. "Do you remember your room number?"

"How can I remember when I never had one?"

"Now *that* line I've heard before," the short man said with a laugh. "Come on now."

Between them the two men herded Jeremy across the room toward the rear door. As they stepped through it Jeremy heard the receptionist say breathlessly, "My, he's in a bad way."

Suddenly the men wheeled Jeremy around so that he faced back into the reception room. The taller of them smiled at the girl. "The doctors will take care of him," he said. He reached out to touch a switch on the wall near the door. The door slid shut.

Beneath his feet Jeremy felt the floor lurch. He was in an elevator, a very small one that began wobbling noisily as it rose. Squashed in between the two men, he soon began to have a sick, suffocating feeling. When, after what seemed an interminable ride, the car stopped and the door opened, Jeremy fell dizzily forward. He would have hit the floor if the men hadn't caught him and pulled him to his feet.

They began walking down a broad well-lighted corridor. It was empty and clean and smelled like . . . like a *hospital*. Jeremy's stomach contracted with a shudder of fear and he pulled back, but the two men hustled him along, past rows of closed and numbered doors until they came to an intersection in the corridor. In the middle of it was a large round desk with a hole in the center. Here in a chair sat another woman in green. She was much older than the receptionist and her face was etched with harsh lines.

"Is this the one?" she demanded.

The tall man nodded and began to repeat the receptionist's story. His voice echoed down the empty corridor.

85*

Jeremy wondered if there were any people behind all those closed doors.

"They're all gone, you know," the woman said, and he was startled. But she was talking to the guard. "All rehabilitated and sent home. He shouldn't be here at all." She eyed Jeremy distastefully. "Number twenty-eight is ready," she said, handing the man a key.

They walked on down the corridor, past the silent numbered doors. When Jeremy cleared his throat, it sounded very loud and both men looked down at him.

"Who lives in these rooms?" he asked. The men exchanged glances.

"You should know," the shorter one said.

"If I did I wouldn't ask," Jeremy snapped. He was fed up with being shunted about like a half-wit or a criminal. They were opposite room number twenty-six when he stopped walking, dragging back the arms of the two men.

"Look," he began in what he hoped was a reasonable tone of voice. "I'd like to ask a few questions." The guards smiled coldly and pulled on his arms, but Jeremy dug in his heels. "You'll have to carry me in there, and I'll yell and fight all the way. Bite too," he added.

The tall guard shrugged. "Ask away," he said.

"Why won't you take me to my father?"

The guard shook his head wearily. "The doctors will help you," he said with the same mechanical smile the receptionist had when she said it. He began pushing Jeremy toward room number twenty-eight. Jeremy dragged his feet and twisted about, but he was no match for the two men. He managed to throw the taller man's arm off for a moment, but it did no good. A final shove, and he was in the room.

"Try to rest," the tall guard said. "Dr. Robertson will see you in the morning."

"I don't want to see him. I want to see Dr. Hillis! I mean Professor Hillis! I want my father." Jeremy lunged at the men, but their arms blocked his escape.

"Good idea to get the name right if you're going to pretend to be his son," the short guard said. He spoke mildly, but there was enough laughter in his eyes to make Jeremy lash out at him with his fist.

"I *am* his son," he yelled.

"Well now," drawled the man, fending off Jeremy's hand and shoving him back into the room, "Doctor Hillis will be mighty surprised to hear that, seeing that he's never had nothing but a daughter." Chuckling, he stepped back to close the door.

Jeremy sprang at it, but it slammed shut in his face and he was left standing in the dark with his hands pressed against the wood. The key turned in the lock, and then out in the hall he heard the sound of the guards' steps going away.

He considered banging on the door, but rejected this thought almost as soon as it came. In view of the security measures already taken with him, it was doubtful if anyone would pay attention. He turned around and looked at his prison. As his eyes became accustomed to the semi-darkness, he could make out the shape of a bed against one wall and a tall chest on the other. He went over to the chest, opened each of the empty drawers, and banged them shut again. Finally he kicked the dresser. Then he stumbled across the room to the bed.

Not just a prisoner, but a crazy one to boot! Jeremy sat on the edge of the bed with his head in his hands. It had been stupid, just stupid, to hope that his father would show up in this nightmare. Whoever *this* Hillis was, he didn't even have a son. . . .

And the other doctor who would see him in the morning, who was he? And when was morning? So much had happened that it was a shock to realize that it was still the afternoon of the day they had gone snapper fishing. Jeremy groaned. He wished he hadn't thought of home. Banging his fist in his palm, he flung himself back on the narrow bed and stared up into the shadows.

He was jerked back into consciousness some time later by the sound of a key in the lock. When the door swung open, all he could see in the dimness was a small figure silhouetted against the light in the corridor.

"My goodness, what are you doing here in the dark?" a girl's voice demanded in familiar fussy accents. The room was suddenly flooded with bright light. Blinking rapidly, Jeremy squinted toward the door and saw his cousin Helene standing there. Her hand was on a switch in the wall.

"What would you like? Morning, afternoon? Sunset's nice." She looked at him inquiringly.

Jeremy scowled at her.

"It's about the only way they're ahead of us—lighting, I mean. And they haven't had electricity as long, either.

Just look, Jeremy, isn't this *real?*" She fiddled with the switch until the room was filled with the pinky-gold light of late afternoon. Then she walked over to the bed and sat down next to him.

"I had supper in the dining room with the doctors and everybody, and I heard them talking about the Red Alert. I knew right away it was you."

Jeremy stared at her. Helene was as casually chatty as if they were sitting in the living room on Quaker Path. As a matter of fact, she'd never been quite as relaxed as this before.

"I knew right away what had happened." She smiled smugly.

Jeremy found his voice. "Great!" he said in disgust. "Suppose you tell me." He flopped back on the bed and looked at his cousin distrustfully.

"Maybe I shouldn't." Helene looked down and smoothed the pleats of her green uniform across her knees. "I'm not sure how much you can absorb. The guards said you were behaving in a very unstable manner."

Jeremy bounced up next to her and grabbed her arm. "If you know what's happened, Helene," he said tensely, "you tell me. Tell me right now."

8

Helene settled back against the wall and looked at Jeremy with a superior expression. "Well," she began slowly, obviously relishing his suspense, "to begin with, you're not even on Earth. You're on Terra."

Jeremy nodded. He knew that. Nevertheless, hearing her say it made a shiver run down his spine.

"OK then," he said. "But what's Terra?"

"Terra is Earth's celestial twin," Helene explained in a rather pedantic tone. "Any attempt to locate it on an astronomical map, however, would be futile. It is in a galaxy infinitely removed from yours." Her eyes slid past Jeremy as she began speaking in a soft monotonous way. "Terra is a world of antimatter, part of the transdimensional universe of antimatter. Terra was created at one and the same instant as your planet, which you call Earth and which is composed entirely of particles of matter. The evolution of the two planets was identical up until the time of the emergence of the telepathic sense, in which capacity we are far advanced."

Jeremy frowned at Helene's bemused expression. "What's the matter with you?" he asked. "You talk as though Terra was your planet or something."

"What?" Helene looked at him blankly for a second.

Abruptly she became more businesslike. "Oh no, stupid, I know it's not my planet. Not yet anyway."

"How do you know all this stuff?" Jeremy hated to have to ask her, but unfortunately she appeared to be in a much more knowledgeable position than he was.

Helene smiled. "Dr. Hillis," she said.

"Did he by any chance tell you why some of the people look alike? Not exactly, but enough to drive you crazy."

"Many of the families here are the same—or started out the same. The emergence of telepathy as an actual evolutionary trend was not discovered until shortly after the Last Great War. . . ." Helene was getting that abstracted look on her face again.

Jeremy interrupted her. "What war?" he asked. "Helene?" He shook her arm and at his touch she seemed to shudder into alertness.

"That's the American Revolution, dummy. Every country here has a Last Great War. The fighting sort of eased off as telepathy grew. I guess you don't fight as much when you share the enemy's fear. They *feel* things better than we do."

"I know." Jeremy was silent for a moment, remembering his experience with Harry when he was drowning and his sense later of the feelings of the men on the dock. "I wonder if we'll ever get like that on Earth," he mused.

Helene didn't seem to hear him. "The most wonderful thing is that I can help here on Terra. I want to help. I want to stay here." She turned to him with a mechanical smile. "You will want to stay here too, Jeremy. Wait until Dr. Hillis explains it all to you."

Helene's eyes shone in her pale face with such intensity that Jeremy became uneasy. "You mean you really don't want to go home?" he asked.

"What home?" Helene asked.

There was no use going into *that,* Jeremy thought uncomfortably. For a moment his eyes avoided Helene's; then he thought of something. "What about Teddy?" he asked abruptly.

Helene lowered her head and began nibbling at a fingernail. "He's the only thing I worry about," she said slowly, "knowing their law about pets. I'm afraid Jessica won't take care of him. She might forget about him, not give him food or water." Her voice dropped so low that Jeremy had to bend his head to hear.

"Is Jessica the other girl, the one who looks like you?"

Helene didn't answer, but started shaking her head. "A bird can't live long without water," he heard her murmur.

Something else she'd said suddenly sank in. "What's this law about pets?" he demanded. He had to repeat the question before Helene looked up.

"Why, it's just that pets have been illegal here for over a hundred years. No one on Terra would think of having a pet, not when there are so many more people here to use up the food and water and space. I know a lot about Terra, Jeremy." Helene wrinkled her forehead. "It was funny the way I learned it. You see, when they met me on the island, I didn't know what had happened. Then Dr. Hillis looked at me . . . and *looked* at me . . . and I sort of knew everything all at once: how they need help and how wonderful Dr. Hillis is and everything. . . ."

Helene was going all soft and dreamy again. Jeremy

shook her arm. "What happened to Charlie?" he asked. As her gaze slowly refocused, he tightened his grip.

"Why, Dr. Robertson has him. He'd never seen a house cat before. Instead of destroying him right away, he said he'd like to do some studies on him."

Jeremy leaped to his feet. "Destroy him! Do studies on him! They can't do that. Charlie is . . . is. . . ." His voice ended in a choke.

Helene looked puzzled. "Don't get so excited. Everything will be all right. There's nothing to be afraid of." She smiled at him in that mechanical way again.

Jeremy wanted to shake his cousin until her silly blank eyes came rolling out of her head. He had actually reached out to lay hold of her, when it hit him. His hands dropped. It was all because of Dr. Hillis. Every time she thought about him, she started talking in that funny way. Clearly part of Helene's mind was not her own anymore.

But there was still one thing the doctor couldn't touch— Jeremy was willing to bet on it. He sat down again and forced himself to speak calmly. "Teddy," he said. "Think of Teddy, Helene."

A look of sadness slowly came over her face. "Oh," she said in a little voice, "I hope he's all right."

"Look—the way you feel about Teddy—that's the way I worry about Charlie." Jeremy spoke rapidly, hoping to capture Helene's interest before she changed again. "Please, help me to find Charlie. Please."

Helene nodded. "All right," she said.

Jeremy rose. "Where did they take him?"

"To the biology lab," she told him, standing up but making no move. Jeremy pulled her to the door.

Once out in the hall, Helene seemed to know what to do. They started back down the corridor toward the intersection where the nurse sat in the round desk. Jeremy pulled back when he realized that Helene was going right up to the nurse, but his cousin urged him along.

The nurse looked up. "Are you taking him upstairs?" she asked. Helene nodded and placed the key on the desk. The nurse bent over her record book and they went on.

Jeremy let out his breath. "How did you manage that?"

"I'm supposed to be Jessie Hillis," she told him. "I can go anywhere I want to in the University. Dr. Hillis trusts me the way he does her, his own daughter. . . ." Helene's steps faltered, and she looked at Jeremy doubtfully. "I don't think I should be doing this," she said.

"No, no," Jeremy interrupted. "You promised."

They continued on down the softly lighted corridor until they came to the elevator. Next to it in the wall was a narrow glass panel. Toward the bottom of it was a small bright dot of light. Jeremy studied it for a moment.

"Down or up?" he asked Helene.

She shook her head. "I don't know. Dr. Robertson didn't come all the way up with us." She paused, trying to remember. "He said something about a cross car. Then he got out and we went on up."

Jeremy shrugged, reached out his hand, and touched the glass. At once the ball of light started moving upward. "I think we've called an elevator," he told Helene.

Below them there was a rumbling as the elevator drew near. At the same moment that the ball of light stopped about midway up the panel, a door in the wall slid noisily apart, and an empty elevator car faced them.

"Come on," Jeremy said. "We'll find it somehow." He was not quite as confident as he sounded. The University was a very large building. He was not likely to stumble upon the biology lab by sheer accident. Still, looking was better than waiting around for something to happen, and there was one thing in his favor. So far, they had aroused no one's suspicions. If he could keep Helene on his side, he might be able to figure out a way to escape—after he'd found Charlie.

Helene seemed to be having second thoughts. "Oh dear," she said fretfully as the elevator door closed upon them, "I know this is wrong. I should have told the doctors about you right away."

"Thank heavens you didn't," Jeremy said grimly. He turned around to look at the car. A luminous glass box, perhaps five inches square, protruded about four inches from the wall. Inside it was the skeletal outline of a building. Stepping closer, Jeremy saw that it was a sort of three-dimensional map of the University. Midway up one of the vertical shafts of the building hovered a dot of light.

"I think that's us!" Jeremy cried excitedly to Helene. Tipping his head, he peered into the map from the side. More shafts extended back and out from the intersection where they were.

"Do you know something, I think this darn thing goes sideways as well as up and down," he said in awed tones.

"I don't care," whined Helene. "I know I'm doing the wrong thing. I should never have let you out."

"Shut up," Jeremy said absently. He had discovered a numbered chart to one side of the map. Next to each number was a name. And, yes, in each cubed space of the map, there was a tiny number corresponding to a number on the chart. A three-dimensional map, he mused, was pretty cool, but there was no time to think about it now. The main thing was to find the biology lab.

Jeremy found it under a subheading, *General Science*, in Section Two. He pressed the little button next to the number, and the elevator immediately started to move.

"Watch," he whispered, poking Helene. As the car descended the light dot slid slowly down the shaft on the map. Before they could reach a connecting horizontal shaft they would have to pass through two floors marked *Maintenance*, two dormitories, two classroom floors, and a large tier marked *Offices*.

"When we get here," Jeremy said, placing his finger on the *Office* level, "I'll bet we turn."

Helene, too, became absorbed in following the progress of the light dot. She nodded. "We *will* turn there," she said. "That is where Dr. Robertson got off with the cat. We went up and then over this way." She traced a path above the level they had started at, followed it over to the right, then up again until her finger came to rest on a large cube marked *Residents' Quarters*.

"Here," she said, pressing her finger on a smaller area marked *Hillis*. "Right here is where we were."

Jeremy was beginning to understand why the University building was so massive. Not only were there enough functioning areas to serve a small village, but the elevator-subway system took up a great deal of room between floors and in the outside walls. That was one reason there were no windows—although maybe not the only reason, he thought darkly. Maybe the place was windowless to lessen the chance of anyone's finding out about what went on inside.

At the very top of the shaft on the left was a large cube that didn't seem to have an elevator leading to it. "What's this one?" Jeremy asked. There was a number suspended in its interior, and when he found the name on the chart it said *Total Security Storage*. Next to it a typed slip had been inserted under the glass, "Special Permission Only."

"What do they store there?" he wondered out loud. Something valuable, he supposed, so valuable that just any old elevator couldn't go there. "Look," he began, turning to Helene. She was staring at the elevator map with a troubled expression.

"It's all very strange, Jeremy, isn't it?" she whispered, raising big frightened eyes to his. It was the first time since they'd met on this crazy planet that she had seemed at all scared. Up until this moment the fact that they were a million miles—no, an *infinity*—from Earth hadn't seemed to bother Helene. Jeremy wished he could tell her how scared *he* was, deep down scared with a wild kind of lostness thrown in that made him want to kick and howl.

But he couldn't confide in Helene. At any moment she might revert to the glassy-eyed disciple of Dr. Hillis. The most he could do was try to get some more information out of her while she was in a flexible mood.

"I'm puzzled by something," he began in a casual tone. "How did we get here? I mean, how did we travel?" The shattering explosion on the dock was all that Jeremy could remember.

"We teleported."

"Teleported?" Jeremy stared at her.

"Traveled by thought. There's no other way to come this far. It's the only way possible."

"You mean we just flew through space and . . . and. . . ." Jeremy didn't like to think about it.

"*Came apart* and flew through space," Helene said with a touch of malice. "I've always known I was telepathic. Didn't you know you were?"

Jeremy shook his head dumbly. Oh, there were the card tricks, and sometimes knowing who was at the door or on the telephone before he answered, but that didn't make him anything out of the ordinary. Or did it?

"I knew about you before we met," Helene went on. "I knew you didn't want me to live with you. I knew you hated me." Her eyes grew hard. "Listen, I didn't want to come, you know!"

"It wasn't hard to tell that!" Jeremy shot back. "No, no, wait! I'm sorry. Please tell me one more thing."

Helene folded her arms across her chest and turned to face the door. Her lips were set in a thin line. Jeremy glanced at the moving dot of light on the map. They were almost at the office level now; at any moment they would start the horizontal trip toward the biology lab.

"That girl, Jessie," he said. "She's the one who got us here, isn't she? How did she do it?" If he could learn *that*, he might be able to figure out a way to get back.

Helene looked stonily at the door. The elevator slowed, then lurched, and with a grating rush slid into the horizontal track.

Jeremy pulled Helene around to face him. "You saw her before you came to Stony Point, didn't you? That's why you were so scared that someone was following us! Tell me, isn't that why you were scared?"

"Yes, yes!" Helene cried. "I *was* scared . . . and I kept putting her back somehow, not letting her in to me because I knew she wanted me to go . . . oh, *somewhere* . . . I didn't know where! It wasn't until I'd met you that I made up my mind to go! Anything was better than where I was! And now I'm glad, very glad I came here!"

Helene's face had turned progressively redder as she delivered her angry harangue, and Jeremy could feel his own face getting hot as he prepared to lash back at her. Then, suddenly, Helene changed. Leaning back against the wall of the car, she shut her eyes, as if the expenditure of so much emotion was too much for her. When she opened them, her eyes had a glassy stare.

"You'll see," she said calmly. "You'll be glad you came, too. Wait until you meet Dr. Hillis." She smiled.

She was going to betray him. Jeremy knew that with a certainty that made his blood run cold. The elevator was slowing down; they were almost there. When the door opened he would have to act because Helene had become the enemy again.

The car stopped.

Jeremy made one last effort to reach her. "Teddy," he cried. "You mustn't forget Teddy!"

For an instant something flickered deep in the blue blankness of Helene's eyes. Then the door slid open. Across from them was a wide hallway and then a wall of frosted glass with large black letters on it: *Biology Laboratory*. Beyond the glass Jeremy could see the blurry outlines of people moving about beneath coronas of light.

9

"Don't be afraid," Helene said, *stepping out of the* elevator and beckoning to Jeremy to follow her.

"I'm not," he replied, summoning a smile as he joined her. There was a pneumatic hiss behind him as the elevator door closed; no escape in that direction. He looked quickly up and down the wide hallway. Walls of frosted glass stretched away on either side. About fifty feet down on the right there was a turn in the corridor—but to reach it would take more time than he had.

"The doctors will help you," Helene said, her eyes drifting past him to the figures moving about behind the glass. "Can you say that with me? The doctors will help me, the doctors will help me. . . ." Her speech was becoming drawn-out and indistinct, like a record on too slow a speed.

Jeremy parroted the words along with her and then, exchanging smiles, they started down the corridor toward a door on the right. He let Helene get several feet ahead of him. She never glanced back to see if he was coming; but continued straight on course for the door—like a robot, he thought. But he might be able to use that to good advantage.

The door to the lab was unlocked and Helene walked

right in, apparently satisfied that Jeremy was behind her. In fact, however, he was speeding noiselessly on down the corridor toward the turn. Here another hallway faced him, but just a few feet ahead was a door. It seemed to lead back into the lab section, but no light shone from it and Jeremy quickly slipped inside. Rustlings and chirpings broke out all around him. He was in some kind of a bird room, he thought.

He flattened himself against the wall and tried to remain as still as possible. Gradually the flutter died down. As his eyes became accustomed to the dimness, Jeremy saw that he was in a large room with racks of cages lining the walls. What light there was came from a half-open door at the far end. The sound of voices came from there, Helene's shrill tones rising above the rest.

"He was *so* with me," she cried.

There was a murmur of masculine voices and then footsteps coming closer. Jeremy ducked down behind a cage of wild geese hoping they would give him cover.

Down at the end of the room the door opened and a tall bald-headed man stepped in, followed by Helene. The man shut the door behind them quickly. "Now, Jessica," he began in a querulous way, "are you sure you're not imagining all this?"

"Of course I'm not. I tell you there's a boy here. It's—"

"I *know* there's a boy here. He's one of my own students," the man interrupted angrily. "Is that all you've come to tell me? Really, Jessica!"

"Stop calling me that!" Helene cried. "You know who I am."

101*

The bald man seized her arm. "Yes, I know," he said, "but my assistants do not. Now listen, my girl, you want to help Dr. Hillis, don't you?"

"Yes," Helene breathed.

"Then don't run around spilling out things about 'Earth' and 'boys from Earth.' *Do you hear me?*" The bald man thrust his face into Helene's. "This whole project is top secret and must be kept so until tomorrow."

"Tomorrow." Helene nodded. "Tomorrow I will speak to Jessica. I remember."

"Shhh. . . ." The bald man looked nervously back over his shoulder toward the door. "I think you'd better get back upstairs to your . . . your father. I'll go with you." As Helene turned to go back into the other room, the man whirled her about. "No, not through there again. Come, we'll go out here." They started toward Jeremy. He crouched down behind the geese.

Helene walked like a zombie, he thought, and her face was frozen into an expression of abject submission. Jeremy held his breath until they were out of the room. He wasn't sure what kind of a mess he was in, but he was certain that Helene was in a worse one. At least he still owned his own mind. He made himself sit still until their footsteps receded; then he jumped up and ran to the door. Somehow he had to get out of here, out of this place where they did things to your mind.

His hand was on the doorknob when he remembered: *Charlie*. He'd come here for Charlie, and in his panic he'd almost run off without him. He looked around. All the birds were in an excited state due to the recent passage of

Helene and the bald man through the room. A bit more commotion wouldn't be noticeable right now, he thought, so he ran quickly across the room.

After listening for a moment at the door, he gently turned the knob and peeked inside. Two men were there, moving about and doing something to the cages stacked about the room. These cages were larger and stronger than the ones in the bird room, and all of them contained small mammals of some sort or another: monkeys, goats, some small sleeping deer. Was Charlie in here?

"What was Dr. Robertson so mad at the kid for?" one of the men asked. He hoisted himself up on a table as his companion cleaned under it with a mop.

"Ah, who knows? He's a mean son of a gun anyhow. Who ever knows what he's doing? What's he trying to prove with all the tests on these poor animals?" The other man swabbed angrily at the floor.

"He's trying . . . he's trying to prove. . . ." The man on the table wrinkled his forehead. "He's trying to prove that animals talk without words . . . that they have tel . . . tel . . . *telepathy!*" He brought the word out triumphantly.

The other man leaned on his mop. "Telepathy. Did we ever have that? *Do* it, I mean. I can almost remember something. But it makes my head hurt to think about it." He started in again with his mop. "Anyhow, I don't see the use of any of it. And if I have to stay here much longer listening to these animals howl, I'm going back outside."

"You can't do that." The man on the table leaned forward and placed his hand on the other's shoulder. "Dr.

Hillis wouldn't like it. We're helping Dr. Hillis, remember?"

The man with the mop straightened up. "That's right," he said. "We're helping Dr. Hillis." The two men were silent as they looked at each other. Jeremy watched in disbelief as idiot smiles spread across their faces.

The man on the table rubbed his eyes. "I'm tired," he said. "Almost done?"

The other nodded and they walked over to the door. There was a sharp click and then total blackness.

"Make it moonlight, will you?" Jeremy heard one of the men say, and in an instant the room lightened to silvery twilight. The door closed and the men were gone.

Jeremy waited until he heard the swish of the elevator outside and then he crept in. He went up and down the rows of sleeping—or drugged?—animals, looking for one in particular until, at last, he saw him, curled neatly in a ball at the bottom of a large cage. Was he asleep? Or was it something deeper than sleep? Jeremy dropped to his knees beside the cage. A fly was walking across Charlie's back, pressing down the long guard hairs, but he didn't stir.

Jeremy pressed his face against the bars. "Here kitty-kitty-kitty," he whispered. He had to keep his voice low and at the same time make it sound as normal as possible.

Gleaming slivers appeared between Charlie's eyelids. They widened until, suddenly, yellow eyes were blazing into Jeremy's.

"What a smart cat, what a good boy!" Jeremy murmured. Charlie purred appreciatively and rubbed his head against Jeremy's cheek.

The cage was locked, but these people on Terra didn't know much about cats, Jeremy thought happily. The cage Charlie was in had been made for a much larger animal. Possibly the cat's long fur had deceived them. In any case, Jeremy had seen him squeeze out of tighter spots than this one. He reached in and started to pull Charlie through the bars.

Charlie seemed to know exactly what was expected of him. Turning his head sideways, he eased it through; his left shoulder followed and then, with a little slithery motion, his right shoulder was through too.

Jeremy picked him up and Charlie wound his front legs tightly around his neck. Just for a moment everything seemed to be all right. "We've got to get out of here," he whispered into Charlie's soft fur, and started toward the door. He wondered if he'd been missed. As if in answer to his question, a voice suddenly came out of a metal grill near the door.

"Second Red Alert. Second Red Alert," it said. "Report to stations and search. Report and search." Above the door a red light flashed intermittently. Helene had spoken to Dr. Hillis.

Jeremy opened the door to the hall. It was empty, but there was the sound of an elevator close by slowing down to a stop. Perhaps the lab assistants were returning to "report and search." Jeremy didn't wait to see but ran down to the other end of the hall.

Coming around the corner, he skidded quickly to a stop. At the far end several white-smocked men were running about excitedly. Luckily they were all facing in the other direction and did not see him. Jeremy ducked back into the hallway he'd come from. He was just in time to see the backs of the two assistants disappearing through the door to the lab. The elevator was still open. Jeremy sprinted for it, thrusting his foot into the opening to force it back. The door slid shut behind him.

Now where? Quickly, quickly! He had to take the elevator *some* place. Jeremy thrust his finger at random into the row of buttons. The car began to fall. He leaned back against the wall and gently disentangled Charlie's claws from his shirt front. When he looked at the button he had pressed, he saw that they were going to the library. That sounded like a busy place. Jeremy frowned. Where, where, where? The elevator door might open on any one of these landings and reveal a crowd of doctors, or guards. Then he saw the button marked *Infirmary*. That was where he had been when Helene found him. There were certainly not many people on that floor, and in one of those empty rooms he and Charlie could find sanctuary. Jeremy pressed the button.

At first Charlie seemed frightened as the elevator lurched upward. Soon, however, his natural curiosity came to the fore and he began to explore his surroundings. Along the three inner sides of the car was an extruded ledge; Charlie was soon up on it, picking his way cautiously along. Suddenly he leaped up, landing on the first of a series of shallow steps in the wall. Above the steps, in the ceiling, was a trap door marked *Emergency Exit*.

"Hey, come down from there." They were almost at the infirmary. Outside, Jeremy heard a roaring sound that grew louder and louder. Charlie jumped down into his arms, his eyes wide. The car shook and Jeremy felt a painful pressure in his ears. It was a familiar feeling, however, reminding him of subways at home.

They had passed another car, he guessed as the sound died away and the elevator resumed its normal speed.

They continued on toward the infirmary. When the light dot indicated that they were almost there, the car began to slow down again. In a moment it had come to a grinding halt. Above him in another shaft Jeremy heard the whoosh of an opening door. People were getting out, and in just a few seconds his car would be pulling in at the same landing. There was no way to avoid it.

Jeremy looked up at the trap door. Then, grabbing Charlie, he scrambled up the three steps and pushed. The trap opened and he pulled himself out onto the roof just as the car came to a final stop.

All about him in the damp, stale-smelling air stretched a dimly lighted forest of elevator shafts. Arm-thick ropes dangled like dead vines between the shafts, and somewhere, far below him, Jeremy could hear the throbbing of a great motor.

He forced himself to look away from the abyss. There was a rickety staircase outside the shaft he was in. Tucking a protesting Charlie into the front of his T-shirt, Jeremy climbed from the roof of the elevator onto the stairway. He found he had to cling tightly to the stair rail as the elevator car roared, lurched, and then fell away beneath him. Within the shaft the frayed ropes moved creakily. Jeremy wondered if the people here knew how flimsy this whole arrangement was.

Below him was the infirmary—and above, *above*, was the area known as "Total Security Storage," the place that had no landing marked on the map. It might be a good place to hide if he could somehow get inside.

There was no need to hold onto Charlie. As Jeremy began to climb, the cat fastened himself like a limpet to the inside of Jeremy's shirt. Up and up he went, not daring to look back. The steps beneath his feet were gritty, and little clouds of dust kept rising up to choke him. When at last he passed the place where the horizontal shafts began, he found there was neither a door nor a landing above it, just a blank wall.

Was it only an empty space then, or a big unfinished attic they hadn't got around to? Jeremy was about to start the perilous descent when he noticed a narrow catwalk along the outside of the horizontal shaft. Warily he edged his way across it until he came to another landing. Here the vertical shaft seemed to be constructed of newer wood, and the ropes were strong and light colored. But without the elevator car to activate the mechanism the doors remained tightly sealed. Jeremy crawled carefully out along the catwalk until he was past the landing. A little farther on, he came to a small door in the wall. It had a knob, a regular knob that he could turn and push. In a moment Jeremy was standing inside a small, dimly lighted room. On the floor lay coils of cable and several massive winches. Everything had the dull, dirty look of long disuse.

A door at the other end of the little room opened into a wide empty hall. It was clean and well-lighted, just like the corridors downstairs, and as he turned a corner Jeremy half expected to see the nurse in the round table sitting there waiting for him. She was not, of course. The intersection was just as empty as the rest of the hallway. Two wide doors of frosted glass were the only things of interest in the whole corridor.

At Jeremy's touch the doors swung silently apart, and he went inside. Here the light was even dimmer. He stood blinking for a few seconds before he realized that he was in a vast, high-ceilinged room, big as an auditorium. Up and down in front of him, in straight rows that stretched on into shadowy grayness, were beds.

Jeremy stepped closer. Actually, the beds were large-sized cribs. It was like being in a giant nursery.

Charlie started to growl deep in his throat, and Jeremy patted him absently. There was something very strange about the scene. What would anyone do with hundreds and hundreds of giant cribs? Was this all that Total Security Storage consisted of? He shook his head and started back to the doors.

At that moment he noticed the breathing—soft and uneven in its rhythm, more like a continuous sighing. It came from the cribs.

10*

Something alive lay there in the cribs. Or many some-
things, Jeremy decided as he listened to the way the soft
sighing came from all parts of the room at once.

Charlie began to struggle in his arms and Jeremy put
him down. The cat ran at once to the doors and pressed
himself against them. Jeremy's inclination was to join him
and to leave the strange room, but he felt himself being
drawn to the cribs. Slowly he moved over to the first row.

A cocoonlike bulge showed beneath the white covering.
It was made by the body of a boy about Jeremy's own age,
to judge from the tousled blond head extending above the
bulge. The boy's eyes were closed, his mouth slightly
opened in a relaxed sleeping position. His arms lay straight
along his sides under the covering.

Jeremy frowned down at the boy. What kind of a sleeping arrangement was this, with big children confined to
cribs like babies? He moved closer, leaning on the top
rail of the crib and bending forward to study the boy. Just
seeing someone his own age gave him a feeling of hope.
If he were to awaken the boy, there was a chance that he
would help him.

He shook him gently, but the boy didn't move, nor was
the steady breathing from his parted lips even slightly disturbed. Jeremy shook him harder, and then harder, until

the boy's head wobbled on his neck like a ripe fruit on a branch. Still he didn't waken.

The crib groaned and creaked as Jeremy continued his shaking. With an effort he made himself stop, then reached his hand out to lay it on the boy's forehead. The flesh was damp and cool. Quickly Jeremy pulled his hand away. There was something very wrong with the strange boy—the *way* he was sleeping, so straight and unmussed, as if he hadn't moved since getting into the crib.

Jeremy's gaze traveled on to the next crib, where he saw another white bulge. Another boy was lying there like living stone under a smoothly drawn cover. It was the same in the next crib, and the next. Some were boys, some were girls. All were about thirteen years old. All slept with the same unnatural rigidity.

Jeremy started running now, up and down each aisle, drawn by a strange unwilling compulsion to look into the other cribs. Around him the soft breathing went on undisturbed, scarcely moving the pale open mouths of the children. Soon all the expressionless faces began to look alike, and Jeremy ran back to the entrance where Charlie paced nervously about near the door.

"Let's get out of here," Jeremy whispered hoarsely. Picking up Charlie, he squeezed his solid warmness against his chest for a second and then threw open the door.

It didn't matter where they went, just so it was away from that room. Jeremy ran wildly down the empty corridor, not caring that his sneakers slapped loudly on the tiles. *They,* the ones back there, wouldn't hear him anyhow.

After a while he slowed down and his mind began to

function with more logic. Turning around, he made his way reluctantly back toward the double doors leading into the sleeping chamber of the children. From there he was able to orient himself enough to find his way back to the little storeroom. Once inside, with Charlie still in his arms, he sank down on a big coil of dusty rope.

But he couldn't dispel from his mind the thought of the children. Who were they and what was wrong with them? Endless rows of bodies, motionless, senseless, yet breathing—they were like . . . like larvae. Jeremy shuddered.

Now Charlie stirred restlessly, and Jeremy put him on the floor where he at once began a sinuous dance about Jeremy's ankles. He paused at last and looked up inquiringly.

"Sorry about that," Jeremy murmured. "No dinner for either of us tonight." The last meal they'd both had was the fish fry on Pig Island. He had no way of telling how long ago that was. His stomach told him it was past his usual mealtime, perhaps nine or ten o'clock. He shrugged. What difference did it make? He was too tired to do anything anyhow. . . .

Jeremy's head drooped forward, snapping up with a jerk when he felt Charlie jump into his lap. "Can't sit up," Jeremy muttered. He slid slowly off the coil of rope onto the floor, where he instantly fell into the deep sleep of exhaustion with Charlie curled in the curve of his arm.

They slept on as a nightful of hours passed. When Jeremy awoke at last, he was conscious of a new sound out in the hall, and he could tell by the alert set of Charlie's ears that he had heard something too. Sliding noiselessly across the floor, Jeremy reached the door and pressed his ear to it. There was a muffled rumbling sound in the hall as if rubber wheels were passing along the tiled floor.

Jeremy heard a voice. "Twenty gallons. Correct. You may pass." The voice was flat and harsh.

A few minutes more went by, during which Jeremy didn't dare even wiggle to relieve his cramped position for fear of missing something. Then he heard another rumble.

"Sheets," droned the flat voice. "Ten gross. Shirts. Five gross. Correct. You may pass." The sound of the wheels resumed and then slowly died away as the wagon, or whatever it was, passed on down the hall.

Jeremy waited for a while, and when there were no more sounds, he opened the door and peeked out. Immediately a steamy food smell flooded in on him and his head reeled. Below him, Charlie's nose wedged itself through the crack in the door. Jeremy pushed him back.

"Wait," he said. "Wait. Let me find out what's going on."

Down at the far end of the corridor, where the doors opened into the crib room, Jeremy saw two long white-enameled tables with big rubber wheels. They stood across from each other on either side of the doors. One of the tables was piled high with what appeared to be folded linen. But it was the other table that drew Jeremy's attention. From a huge shiny vat rose a steamy mist that seemed to carry with it the foody smell. Jeremy's stomach rumbled.

There was no one in sight. Suddenly the risks seemed slight compared to the extent of his hunger. Near the coil of rope was a rusty can half full of nails. Jeremy picked it up and dumped out the nails. Then he wiped the inside of the can with the tail of his shirt.

"You wait here," he said, pushing Charlie back from the door. Slipping into the hall, Jeremy ran toward the tables. The steaming mess of gray-white porridge wasn't very appetizing, but he was in no mood to be fastidious. Next to the vat lay a large ladle with a shallow pouring spout on one end. He filled it with porridge, poured it into the can, and then ran back to the storeroom.

He shut the door behind him and leaned against it panting for a second before examining his prize. Then he sat down on the coil of rope. *Ugh*! Jeremy had never liked hot cereal and this was even slimier than most. Nevertheless, he raised the can to his lips and took a swallow. It was too hot and was rather tasteless, but it *was* food. Soon he was gulping it down. Only with an effort was he able to save some at the bottom of the can for Charlie. Cleaning a spot on the dusty floor he poured it out for him.

Charlie sniffed at it once, turned up his nose, and began washing his paws with a great show of indifference. Jeremy watched him worriedly. Animals always knew, people said. Maybe the stuff was really some kind of poison. Who was it for anyhow? Jeremy had an idea about that, and he opened the door again and peeked out.

Two men in green uniforms were down at the other end of the hall. As Jeremy watched they each got behind one of the big carts. The swinging doors had been pushed back and Jeremy could see into the room beyond. Now what . . . ? Jeremy's heart began to beat faster as he saw movement in the cribs. The children were getting up and swinging their legs stiffly over the lowered sides of the cribs. One by one they arose. When they were all up, they began moving slowly toward the center of the room, where they formed an orderly line.

The line moved silently forward until the first boy reached the table with the vat of porridge. The waiting guard raised the dipper from the vat and the boy tilted back his head. The contents of the dipper poured into his mouth and he went on, turning to the other table with scarcely a break in pace. Here he held out his arms. Two pieces of folded white cloth were placed in them and he moved on. A few steps farther, and he made a precise turn, then walked on down the intersecting corridor and out of sight.

Meanwhile the whole procedure was repeated by the next boy. Jeremy watched in horrified fascination as the line moved slowly forward. The children's eyes were open now, but their faces were just as vacant of expression as when they had been sleeping. They moved woodenly, and they spoke not at all.

There was something mechanical about the movements of the attendants too. Although their mouths were closed and their heads turned occasionally from side to side, they wore looks of blank indifference. They *did* speak however—little clipped remarks such as "Correct" and "Check" as the line passed them—and all of it in contrast to the appalling silence of the children.

A girl with curly dark hair came up to the porridge vat, startling Jeremy with her resemblance to Jean Albert, a girl in his class at home. Up went the ladle—but it missed its mark. No one noticed, and the girl passed on to the linen table with a cup of steaming gruel running down the front of her shirt.

Jeremy had seen enough. Closing the door, he leaned back against the wall. He was feeling somewhat sick and wished now that he had not eaten the gruel. At his feet Charlie sat looking up at him with an expectant air.

"I don't know what to do now," Jeremy told him. No matter where he went he was faced with new evidence of Dr. Hillis's strange power. This last thing—those mindless children out there—was the worst. Jeremy's mind went round in circles as he tried to think of a way to escape.

For a long time he sat and stared at Charlie as he thought. There was only one answer: find a way to go home. But where was home from Terra? There was no road, no air flight map to show him which way to go. The only link between Earth and Terra was the tenuous connection between the minds of the two girls, Helene and the other one, Jessica Hillis. How he had become mixed up in this Jeremy wasn't sure, unless it had something to do with Helene and himself having some of the same genes and being telepathic toward each other.

Jeremy groaned and wished again he'd never heard of his cousin. Nevertheless, she was his only hope now. "Tomorrow I'll speak with Jessica," she had told Dr. Robertson. Tomorrow was *today*. If he could find Helene and see how she established the contact with Jessica, perhaps he could do it too. It was a slim chance, but it was all Jeremy could think of.

He couldn't take Charlie with him, though. With the cat along, he wouldn't have the freedom of movement he needed. The little storeroom might well become Charlie's tomb. Jeremy stretched out his hand and passed it quickly over the round, familiar shape of Charlie's skull, lingering briefly to scratch the hollow spots at the base of his ears. Then he stood up and walked over to the door to the elevator shaft. Without looking back, he opened it and stepped out onto the catwalk.

As the musty air of the shaft closed about him, Jeremy let out a long shaky breath. From what he remembered of the map Dr. Hillis's apartment was two levels down and then over to the left . . . or was it the right? In any case, *down* was the first way to go. Jeremy looked just once; the semidarkness below him melted into an inky chasm of stomach-lurching depth.

Keeping his eyes fixed on the section of catwalk immediately in front of him, he started to walk toward the stairs. Then he began the descent. Down he went, hand over hand, never looking below him. Twice elevator cars rushed past, and he had to cling tightly to the wooden steps to avoid being shaken off. Then at last he was at the level he wanted, and now Jeremy had to decide whether the residents' quarters were to his right or to his left.

Crouching in the gloom above the landing he tried to reconstruct the map more precisely in his mind. Soon he noticed that the elevator cars passing him were all heading in the same direction—to the right. Could they be going to Dr. Hillis's office too? "Top Secret until tomorrow." Dr. Robertson's words came back to him with new meaning. Whatever Dr. Hillis's plan for Helene was, perhaps it was about to be told to the world today! It was a plausible theory.

Since Jeremy had just about decided that right was the

direction he wanted anyhow, he started along the horizontal catwalk. Here the rushing cars sped by like subway trains.

Half an hour later he was sitting on the catwalk above a landing in the second section. By now he was certain he was in the right spot. Elevators had been steadily discharging passengers below him, and in the faint sound of voices penetrating upward to his hiding place he could detect an air of excitement.

At last one car came, discharged its passengers, and then, contrary to what the other cars had done, did not move on but remained at the landing platform. Apparently it was the last car.

Jeremy peered down the tracks in both directions and then up and down. No flickers of light, no singing along the tracks indicated the approach of more cars. The time had come for him to crash the party.

He climbed over onto the roof of the elevator car and lowered himself through the trapdoor. His feet thudded heavily on the floor of the car when he dropped, and for a moment he crouched there tensely, waiting to see if he'd been heard. Outside everything remained quiet, but he had no way of knowing what lay beyond the closed door to the elevator. Armed guards might be there . . . or one of the doctors. On the wall in front of him near the door was a button marked *Open*. Jeremy took a deep breath and pressed it.

With a soft hiss, the door slid open and he looked out into . . . a garden! He could hear birds twittering and could see golden light filtering onto the red brick paving. It reminded him of the restored colonial gardens at home. For a moment the feeling of being in a dream came rushing

118*

back, and Jeremy had to give himself a mental shake. A closer look revealed large stone pots holding the trees, and cages holding the birds. The illusion of being outdoors vanished.

Jeremy peered cautiously around the door of the elevator. The garden room appeared to be long and narrow. There was a latticed doorway at one end, where moving shadows indicated the presence of people on the other side. He darted out of the elevator and hid behind a tiered bank of philodendrons near the latticed door. As he crouched there, heart pounding, he heard a familiar voice.

"I don't want to do it. I'm afraid." The voice was high and strained and it cracked a bit on the last word, but Jeremy had no trouble identifying it as Helene's.

"You'll do it." This was a man's voice, cold and hard. Jeremy parted the leaves and saw Dr. Robertson and Helene walking slowly down the brick path toward him. Except for a splotchy redness around the eyes, Helene was very pale. Dr. Robertson's big hand was closed tightly around her upper arm. She kept glancing down at his hand with a trapped expression.

Fear suddenly streamed from her to Jeremy, just the way it had the other two times. But now the impact was more direct, as if being on this telepathic planet had somehow sharpened his perceptions. Shutting his eyes, Jeremy clutched the ropy stems of the plants for support. He told himself firmly that the fear was not *his* . . . not *his* . . . not *his*. In a moment the dizziness passed and he was able to view the scene more calmly.

From the other end of the room a man was walking toward Helene and Dr. Robertson. He was tall and slightly stooped with a head of heavy brindle-colored hair. The close-cropped beard beneath his chin had a distinctly orange cast to it. *Dad.*

The word formed in Jeremy's mind but luckily did not reach his lips, for as the man came closer he saw that it was not his father. Taken feature for feature, he resembled him, to be sure, but it was the kind of resemblance that is known as "family." This man's face was coarser; deep lines ran down from his tight lips. It could only be Dr. Hillis.

"Ah there, Doctor." Still holding tightly to Helene's arm, Dr. Robertson turned and beckoned to the other man. "We're a bit reluctant today, I'm afraid."

Dr. Hillis quickened his steps until he stood next to them. "Reluctant? How is that?" Beneath the purring tone, Jeremy detected a steel-like quality. Dr. Hillis put his arm around Helene's shoulders. "Now, you'll help us today, won't you, Helene?" He smiled down at her.

"Yes," Helene breathed.

"Remember what I told you?"

Helene's face lighted up. "Of course," she said, smiling foolishly.

Exchanging satisfied glances, the two men guided Helene along the path toward the door.

11

They were coming straight toward him! Jeremy's breathing quickened until the philodendron leaves near his face trembled wildly. He tried to hold his breath, but that had the opposite effect of making him breathe even more rapidly. He soon saw that it didn't matter anyhow. Totally engrossed in soft-voiced conversation with each other, the two men walked along without the slightest suspicion that they might be observed. Helene, between them, was in a glassy-eyed trance.

Jeremy leaned forward as much as he dared, trying to catch some of the conversation.

"Is *he* there?" Dr. Hillis asked his companion.

Running his tongue over his lips, Dr. Robertson nodded eagerly. "He's there all right, front row center," he said. They were so close now that Jeremy could see the little drops of moisture in the corners of his mouth. "Your opposition's there too," he added sourly. "Over on the left."

Dr. Hillis smiled. "No problem. When they find out what we have here, there'll be no more questions."

Just then one of the caged lovebirds above them let out a squawk, quite unlike the soft cooing of its fellows. Helene came to a sudden stop. Head up, her eyes anxiously searched the upper branches of the trees.

"Teddy," she breathed.

Angrily she tore her arm from Dr. Robertson's grasp and pressed her hand to her head. "What am I doing?" she cried.

"I told you it wouldn't last!" Dr. Robertson turned to Dr. Hillis with a panicky look. "It gets shorter each time."

Dr. Hillis frowned, then looked quickly around the room. "Be quiet," he told the other man. "Now, Helene, look at me. Give me your hands."

"No, no, I won't!" Helene's blond hair whipped about as she shook her head. "I won't do that again!"

"Seize her," Dr. Hillis ordered curtly.

"You could be killed for this," Jeremy heard Dr. Robertson mutter. Nevertheless, he grabbed hold of Helene's arms and twisted them behind her back until she was facing the other doctor.

"Now raise your head," ordered Dr. Hillis.

Helene stared stubbornly at the floor. "I won't," she said.

Dr. Hillis roughly jerked Helene's chin up. "Look at me."

The fear that came to Jeremy from his cousin was like a palpable thing that wrenched his mind about; he *felt* her terror, *felt* her resistance. Helene struggled for a moment, but finally her eyes glazed and she sagged down into Dr. Robertson's arms.

Waves of anger rose in Jeremy, washing away his dislike of his cousin and leaving only pity for her. Just wait, he thought, clenching his teeth, I'll get you out of here, I'll get us *both* out of here.

There was a sound of harsh breathing, and for a moment

122*

Jeremy was afraid that it was his, and that he would be discovered. But it came from Dr. Hillis, who was holding Helene in the fiercely concentrated power of his cold eyes.

"There," he said at last. "That will do. Just enough and not too much . . . not yet." His face was white, and he took a handkerchief from his pocket to wipe the perspiration off his forehead.

"You took a terrible chance doing that right out here in the open. Anyone might have come along," said Dr. Robertson.

"It had to be done." Straightening his shoulders, Dr. Hillis again steered Helene toward the door. This time she offered no opposition. They disappeared into the room beyond.

Jeremy crept along the floor until his face was up against the frame of the doorway. It was worked in the same open pattern as the door itself and provided several small peepholes into the other room. He pulled the bushes carefully over his head and shoulders and looked inside.

The door was at the back of a large room—or a small auditorium, to judge from the rows of seats on either side of a center aisle. Helene and the two doctors were halfway down the aisle. As they advanced, heads turned to watch them.

At the front of the room was a dais with a large semicircular table on it. Beyond the dais red and yellow lights played on the bare wall like flames. As Helene and the doctors mounted the steps, two men already sitting at the table stood up. At the same time Dr. Hillis inclined his head toward someone in the front row.

123*

"Mr. President," he intoned, his voice booming out in the silence. Then he took Helene's arm and went around to the other side of the table, where they sat down.

President of what? Jeremy wondered. He didn't wonder for long. Dr. Robertson stepped forward and addressed the crowd.

"Honored President of the United States," he began. Jeremy pressed his ear closer to the peephole.

"Senators, congressmen, members of the press, fellow scientists." Dr. Robertson's voice had a breathy way of running down and Jeremy found it difficult to follow him. If he did not keep his ear pressed to the peephole he could not hear him very well. On the other hand, if he wanted to *see* him, he had to give up listening when he put his eye to the hole.

Robertson was obviously making some sort of introductory speech. Filled with many such phrases as "a man who" and "a man with," it had the laudatory tone of the college invocation speeches Jeremy had heard so often. He pressed his eye to the peephole.

There were several hundred people in the room. Would any of them believe his story? he wondered. They looked like ordinary Earth-type people, but they weren't, Jeremy told himself. His best hope lay in remaining hidden and trying to find out all he could about the process that linked Terra to his home planet.

Turning his attention back to Dr. Robertson, he realized that he had missed part of his speech. Now, smiling toothily, the doctor was gesturing toward the table. ". . . I give you Dr. William Hillis."

As Dr. Hillis stepped forward applause began. It was sporadic rather than wildly enthusiastic, and Jeremy felt an irrational burst of hope.

Just then there was a swish behind him as the elevator door opened. Jeremy's head spun around. Four young women in green walked in. With them were two uniformed guards. One of them was the tall man who had shoved him into his prison room. Jeremy ducked behind the philodendrons as the group approached. At the door they stopped. One set of green legs was only inches from Jeremy's hiding place.

"You girls sneak in. We'll watch from out here," he heard a male voice say. The door opened and the girls went in.

Jeremy looked up. Leaning back against the wall, one of the guards was lighting a cigarette. The other had his face pressed to the latticework at one side of the door.

Jeremy's heart pounded in his ears. It seemed impossible that the guards didn't hear it too. Very slowly he twisted around until once more he faced his own peephole under the bushes.

Dr. Hillis was saying something about the "staggering problems of an overcrowded planet." Jeremy had no trouble hearing *him*.

"We here at the University," the vibrant voice went on, "have struggled for years to remedy these problems. We have studied the resources of land and sea, of the animal world and the human world, attempting to discover means of development to support our teeming multitudes. The cultivation of marine life here at Stony Point has been one

125*

of our outstanding successes." Applause at that. Dr. Hillis held up his hand.

"Two years ago I was awarded a grant from our President to conduct a survey of young people on the threshold of maturity in the hopes of discovering sources of untapped scientific genius. Well, gentlemen, I discovered more than that. Far, far more."

Dr. Hillis paused and let his gaze roam about the audience. On the wall behind him the red and yellow lights writhed like snakes of fire. The room was very still.

Suddenly there was a commotion on the left side of the room, as a small dark-haired man jumped to his feet. "Just a minute, Hillis," he cried. "What *about* those young people? There's a rumor that a lot more came in here than ever went out!"

Luckily, the guards had become engrossed in the action inside the auditorium or they would have surely seen the bushes shake as Jeremy slapped his fist into his palm. Go on, go on! he urged the little man silently.

On the dais, Dr. Robertson banged on the table. "Silence, silence!" he demanded piercingly.

Dr. Hillis cut him off with a firm gesture. "A rumor only, Senator DeWitt," he said smoothly. "The majority of the young people interviewed returned to their homes. The parents of the few who elected to stay receive weekly reports from their children. My colleague in this project can testify to that. Is that not so, Dr. Robertson?"

The other doctor nodded.

"And now, may I proceed with my announcement? It is surely the most exciting one in the history of Terra!" He looked out over the crowd, and there were cries of "Yes!" and "Hear, hear!" To Jeremy's intense disappointment, Senator DeWitt sat down.

Dr. Hillis waited until the room was perfectly quiet and then he began to speak. "Gentlemen, what we have discovered is not just one scientific genius, not two, not three, but an entire world of scientific geniuses! We have discovered an entirely new planet."

There were gasps of surprise in the audience, and as heads turned to each other, Jeremy saw several raised eyebrows.

"The bridge to this new world is telepathy—not just the limited telepathy many of us enjoy, but a strengthened and amplified power known as teleportation. Yes, I have discovered a way to transport a material body through the chasms of space to this new world solely through the power of the mind.

"You ask how this can be?" Dr. Hillis's voice sank to hardly more than a whisper, but the air in the room seemed electrically charged to carry it to the very last row and beyond—right out to the three listeners in the hall. "It can be because your trust and faith in our work here has enabled us to devote our entire lives to the success of this project: Project *Earth*!"

A shiver went down Jeremy's spine as the word *Earth* was repeated around the room. The murmur rose, becoming mixed with applause. On the dais one of the men was openly weeping. Jeremy shut his eyes against the look of triumph on Dr. Hillis's face.

Then in the midst of the clamor he became aware of one

127*

voice rising above the rest. He opened his eyes to see Senator DeWitt on his feet again, waving his clenched fist in the air.

"Proof, proof!" he cried, his face darkly flushed. He ran across the front of the room toward the dais.

Near Jeremy the latticed doors swung open as the two guards slipped into the room. In a moment they were hurrying down the aisle.

"Mr. President." The Senator turned to the man in the front row. "I . . . I . . ." he faltered as the guards approached him. "I demand an investigation," he finished defiantly.

Here and there in the room, others had taken up the cry of "Proof!" Jeremy jumped to his feet. In a moment he would have been inside, adding his voice to the others, if just then Dr. Hillis hadn't made another announcement.

"*I have proof,*" he proclaimed in ringing tones. From somewhere he produced a small black box, which he now held up. "Here is your proof!" he cried. He continued to hold the box above his head while the audience grew quiet and the guards hustled Senator DeWitt back to his seat. Then, flourishing his arm like a magician, he opened the box.

He took out something flat and shiny. Whipping it about in the air he unfolded it to reveal a shimmering rectangle of transparent material. Handing the box back to Dr. Robertson, he proceeded to stretch the material out still more; then he held it up in front of him.

Jeremy recognized it, and sank back on his knees in bewilderment. It was the plastic bread wrapper his father had given to Helene for the jingle shells. But—what was so great about that?

Dr. Hillis began to explain. "Gentlemen," he said solemnly, "there is no such material as this existing anywhere on Terra."

He walked over to the table and pointed to the two men seated on the other side of Helene. "Doctors, last night you ran extensive tests on this material. It is a by-product of coal tar, is it not?" The two men nodded.

Dr. Hillis came forward on the platform. "It is, in fact, the very product sought by scientists in one of our most highly endowed projects—the DeWitt Project." He looked over at the little senator.

"But . . . but . . . that's *secret* research," DeWitt protested. His voice was noticeably weaker, however, and he kept to his seat.

Dr. Hillis waved the bread bag about. "On Earth, Senator, this product is so cheaply made and so abundantly produced that it is used to package common items of food. This, my friends, is a bread wrapper—a bread wrapper from the planet Earth."

There was absolute silence in the room. Dr. Hillis quickly beckoned Helene forward.

"Further proof of my claim, gentlemen, will be provided shortly when this girl you see here, who is from Earth, makes contact with her home planet." He pulled Helene closer to him and smiled down at her.

The look of happy compliance on his cousin's face made Jeremy feel sick.

12

Dr. Hillis leaned forward solicitously. "Are you ready?" he asked Helene. When she nodded, he reached into his pocket and pulled out a gold watch on a chain.

"Ten o'clock," he announced. "Ten o'clock on the morning of Saturday, June twenty-third. Here—and on Earth!" His voice vibrated with meaning. "Gentlemen, you are about to witness history!"

Not a murmur or a rustle disturbed the tense silence of the auditorium. Helene began to speak in a slow, clear voice.

"I am waiting to contact Jessica Hillis." She paused. "My mind is open."

There was a little click somewhere behind Jeremy's eyes. He was suddenly dizzy as a reeling void seemed to open up around him. He clutched the latticework with both hands and held on.

In a moment things steadied down, and he found that he was still there, under the bushes outside the crowded auditorium. The only difference was that the top of his head seemed to remain suspended in the whirling dark of the void. Soon little wavering lines of light, vague pictures, and finally a voice came into the blackness.

Jeremy saw Helene's lips move, and he realized that the voice he heard was hers. At least it sounded like hers. But it synchronized with the one he heard in his head too. With the part of his mind that functioned apart from the whirling black, Jeremy became aware that it was not Helene's thought that was being expressed. The sound was hers, the vocal cords and the breath behind the sound were hers, but the words themselves were transmitted directly from a mind a myriad of galaxies away—the mind of Jessica Hillis. It was Jessica talking into the minds of both of them. Fascinated, yet terrified by what was happening, Jeremy remained frozen against the doorframe as Jessica-Helene continued.

"And also the information you requested about hydroponics"—the girlish voice stumbled over the word—"and the chemical food supplements—vitamins they are called. And, oh yes, you were right, there are many synthetic fabrics and construction materials. When the memory banks are present I will transmit full reports. The University here has a library that is more than adequate."

Jessica-Helene grew quite enthusiastic. Jeremy watched his cousin's face mirror the change. Then, suddenly, her mouth shut and her face went blank. Jeremy blinked. The *voice* had not stopped. It continued in his head.

"Secret message for my father. Do not vocalize. The visual communication you asked about is a *fact*. Television, they call it. Information concerning its construction is freely available."

The voice stopped, really stopped this time, and after a moment the blackness at the top of Jeremy's head disappeared. He shook it gently. All his again—and what a relief that was!

Up on the dais Helene's slight figure looked smaller

than ever as she took a stumbling step backward toward the table. Dr. Hillis guided her to her chair.

Meanwhile, the audience had come to life, and voices took up the words *hydroponic* and *vitamin* and *synthetic* with increasing excitement. Dr. Hillis held up his hand for silence.

"This is only the beginning," he proclaimed oracularly. "Only the beginning."

A sort of lassitude had come over Jeremy. The voices in the auditorium were scrambling together. Eyes half shut, he let himself slide down against the doorframe.

"Benefits . . . people of Terra . . . new world. . . ." Dr. Hillis's voice still dominated the others, but it had become increasingly harder to follow him. "Era of plenty . . . powers of Earth . . . Earth . . . Earth. . . ."

With a tremendous effort of will Jeremy pulled himself out of his torpor. Looking up at the dais he saw that Helene had succumbed to the same fatigue. She lay slumped forward across the table, with her head on her arms. Dr. Robertson shook her.

"Mr. President!"

Jeremy came fully awake as he heard the clear, hard tones of Senator DeWitt.

"That child is not well!"

From the front row came a rumble of sound, and then a tall young man stood up. His voice was high and rather soft. "President requests . . . assurances . . . no harm. . . ." Jeremy could only make out a few of the words, but whatever else was said, none of it ruffled Dr. Hillis's composure.

"She is tired, that is all. No harm has been done." He turned toward the table. "Are you feeling quite well now, my dear?"

Helene lifted her head. She didn't answer right away but thrust her hand through her hair while her mouth fell open in a yawn. Jeremy found he had to yawn too.

"I'm not so tired now," he heard her say.

Nor was he. The fatigue was passing and with the return of strength came a memory of something important, something . . . secret. What? Jeremy frowned.

Senator DeWitt was still speaking. "Two things more, Dr. Hillis," he said. Jeremy wanted to cheer the little man's persistence. "First, what are these memory banks?"

"Simply a term we use to describe the phenomenal memories of some of our telepathic young people here at the University," Dr. Hillis said smoothly. "They are a few boys and girls who elected to stay and receive such information as might be telepathically transmitted. A laudable decision, Senator, one prompted by patriotism, and one for which these brilliant young people will be suitably rewarded."

A pleased murmur rose in the crowd, but Jeremy was horrified. He knew as clearly as if the doctor had shouted it that these "brilliant" young people were the ones in the cribs.

Senator DeWitt stroked his chin in silence for a moment. "Second thing," he said. "I challenge you, Dr. Hillis!" His voice rose and Jeremy saw the two guards step forward. "I challenge you to submit the young lady to a Prober test!"

133*

"Prober!" Dr. Robertson fairly shouted the word as he leaped to his feet.

"Prober, yes." Dr. Hillis took it up smoothly. "Of course, that has always been our ultimate test for truth. But it might, at this time, disturb the delicate mental contact between our two telepaths. However, Mr. President, if you authorize me to take the risk. . . ." He shrugged.

There was more of the rumbling murmur in the front row; then the young aide got to his feet again. "The President submits . . . too great a risk." He sat down.

"Thank you for your confidence, sir," Dr. Hillis said, bowing to the President. "And now," he said, his voice growing louder, "before we adjourn the meeting until tomorrow morning at ten, there is time for a brief discussion of the discoveries hinted at in the recent contact with Earth."

A buzz of comment arose in the audience, and Jeremy saw a dozen hands go up. Dr. Hillis has won, he thought dully. There was no one left who would believe him, no one willing to jeopardize the exciting future the doctor held out for Terra. Jeremy twisted his head about trying to see what had become of Senator Dewitt. Back in his chair, the little man had slumped down; only the top of his head was visible. The two guards stood close behind him. Now, as Jeremy watched, they began to walk toward the back of the room. He shrank down inside his clothes. In a moment they would be out in the hall again and his chance of leaving would be cut off. Half crawling, half running, Jeremy hurled himself across the room toward the elevator.

He let out a long shaky breath as the door closed on

him. He was safe, for the moment. He turned to the back of the car to study the map. He had to get out of the University and find Harry. Harry had said he was a Prober. According to what he'd just heard, Probers were important people. Harry would be able to help.

He decided to direct the car over to the next horizontal level, get out, and climb up the catwalk to the Total Security unit where Charlie was. Then he and Charlie would get out of the building somehow.

Or would they? Jeremy had a sudden vision of himself climbing down endless steps in the dark with a possibly protesting cat in his shirt front. It would take time, if it worked at all. And wasn't this perhaps the only moment when the front entrance might be unguarded? From what he'd seen of the people in the auditorium, most of the personnel of the University was there.

Even as he agonized over his decision, Jeremy heard steps out in the hall and a rising sound of voices. They were coming out of the auditorium! Quickly he reached out and pressed the button: *Ground Floor, Reception Desk.*

I'll get you soon, he promised Charlie silently as the car sped downward. But in his heart he knew Charlie was lost to him forever. It was some consolation to know that, at least, the cat was no longer in the biology lab.

Just as he'd hoped, the reception room was empty. In a moment Jeremy was out in the narrow dark passage facing the heavy wooden door with its tiny square of dark frosted glass—where he had come in yesterday—and where he *should* be able to get out, he told himself five minutes later, after failing to find any way at all to open the great door.

135*

Pounding and pushing did no good, and there was no handle anywhere on the smooth surface.

Yet the receptionist had opened it. Jeremy raised himself up and peered through the tiny square of glass the way he imagined she had done. To his surprise, he could see outside quite clearly. The sun was shining.

Yesterday he'd been standing out there and she had been in here. Then he had knocked, and waited. Why had he waited, even after he'd been seen?

Because the control for the door was not here, but somewhere else!

Jeremy ran back to the desk and, sure enough, on the wall next to the telephone apparatus was a simple switch marked *Door*. Two buttons, labeled *O* and *C*, made the whole thing crystal clear. In a few seconds he was out in the sunshine.

Harry had said, "You know where I live," as if he knew Jeremy would need him again. Jeremy started running down the road toward the village. He was almost there when he saw that he did not have to go to Harry's house. Marching across the square toward the dock was a platoon of yeomen, with Harry's red head plainly visible above the others.

13*

"*Harry!*" *Jeremy started calling his name as he ran through* the quietly idling crowd in the square. He paid no attention to the curious looks he received, but kept on until he reached the big man's side.

"You've got to help me!" He paused for breath. He would have gone on if Harry hadn't lifted his hand warningly.

"Wait," he said, looking over Jeremy's shoulder at the University. Jeremy looked too and saw a group of green-uniformed guards coming out of the entrance.

Get in among the yeomen. Harry's thought flooded into Jeremy's head and he quickly complied.

"Eyes front." This order was given in loud clear tones. The yeomen reluctantly left off staring at Jeremy and resumed their march. Jeremy walked with his head lowered, but just before they reached the end of the dock he looked back. Two of the guards were now standing on the steps below the Hercules monument, turning their heads slowly as they surveyed the crowd.

At the end of the dock a dozen or more rowboats were moored. Again an unspoken command came to Jeremy, and he hurried down the ladder. Once in the rowboat, he lay on the floor. A moment later a fishy-smelling canvas came down over him and the boat began to move.

For Jeremy, lying hot and cramped beneath the canvas, the steady rowing went on for an uncomfortably long time. Finally the canvas was lifted.

"Don't sit up yet," Harry, in the seat just in front of him, warned. "We're still not out of sight."

Jeremy nodded and lay still as the boat continued its steady progress. Two yeomen were sitting in the stern and one in the rowing seat next to Harry. Their eyes sparkled as they glanced down at Jeremy. Waves of curious feelings came to him from the boys until he grew very uncomfortable. He wanted to explain his unusual situation to them, but each time he looked up at Harry and would have spoken, he felt a warning from the older man flood his mind: *not yet*. Jeremy closed his eyes.

"Here we are," Harry said at last as the boat bumped onto wood. Jeremy knew it was all right for him to sit up now. Next to them was the straight side of a great flat barge, riding almost motionlessly on the small choppy waves. They were nearly into Long Island Sound, at a point about midway between the two land arms of the harbor.

All along the side of the barge the yeomen were tying their dinghies to cables that stretched down from the deck. They seemed to know what to do, and after a few brief instructions to them about the direction of the current, Harry was able to turn his attention to Jeremy.

"Tired, are you? Cramped, I wouldn't be surprised." Harry reached a helping hand down from the deck as Jeremy crawled up the rope ladder.

"I'm all right," he said as Harry led him toward a little wooden house that sat like a box in the center of the barge. Two rusty smokestacks backed up to it.

Inside, Jeremy saw that the little house was both engine room and cabin. Half of the room was devoted to an impressive assortment of gears and levers. The other half contained a narrow bunk bed, a wooden chest, and two rough-hewn stools.

Harry directed Jeremy to the bunk and then went over to the engine. "We'll be underway soon," he said with a reassuring smile. "It's two miles out to the beds, and then the yeomen know what to do."

They couldn't get far enough away from the village to suit him, Jeremy thought as he sank back on the bunk. He watched Harry lean out of the window above the engine to call orders to the boys. Although he could see and hear him, it all seemed to be taking place far away. Slowly Jeremy's eyelids drifted down. . . .

"I wish I could let you sleep." Harry's voice came to him muffled and dreamlike. Jeremy opened his eyes. There was a steaming bowl of something that smelled like clam chowder in Harry's hand. Jeremy reached for it eagerly.

"Go slowly," Harry cautioned as Jeremy raised the bowl to his lips. He stopped obediently for a moment, but then hunger overcame him and he finished the bowl in greedy gulps. He handed it back to Harry.

"How long is it since you've had a meal?" the big man asked.

Jeremy stared at him blankly for a second, then said, "A meal? I had some oatmeal stuff this morning." He swallowed. A sick feeling washed over him as he remembered. "Harry, I need your help," he cried. "You're a Prober and they said a Prober test. We've got to get home again."

Harry held up his hand. "Easy now," he said. "Take it from the beginning. When I left you yesterday you were going to try to find your father."

"My father!" Jeremy exploded. "He's not my father, any more than this is Earth, or you're really Captain Harry or . . . or . . . anything!" His voice rose. All of a sudden it seemed hopeless to be sitting here expecting help from a perfect stranger.

"Wait," Harry said firmly. "Before you go any further, let's talk about this. *I* am real, *you* are real. Terra is real too, and if this Earth you speak of is real, then there must be some logical explanation for it all."

Jeremy nodded. He was in control of himself now. As carefully as he could, he repeated to Harry what Helene had told him about the relationship of Terra to Earth. "And she said that we came here by . . . by teleportation."

Harry didn't seem surprised by the strange word. "Of course," he said. "That would be it. The Probers have known for a long time about teleporting. It's possible that an exchange can be made between two people who are close in a special way. Jessica Hillis and your cousin must be some kind of twins."

"And *me*," Jeremy added grimly. "I'm included. Helene and I have some of the same genes, my father said. Then there's this funny way we're connected in our minds. It's something like the way people are all the time here."

"That is the Greater Sense. You don't have it in your world?"

"No." Then Jeremy added quickly, "At least—well, that's what I *would* have said. But here I am and there's Helene in the University, so I guess some of us have it."

"And possibly the two of you equaled the telepathic identity of Jessica Hillis," Harry mused.

"But why is Charlie here?" Jeremy demanded. When Harry looked puzzled, he explained.

The big man's eyes widened. "A cat? A real old-fashioned house cat? I'd like to see him." He shook his head. "But I don't know why he's here too, unless—was he in your cousin's arms perhaps?"

Jeremy hooted. "She hates cats. But he might have been touching her. He followed her around, trying to be cute or something. When that fog moved in, he was practically sitting on her feet. It's all so crazy."

"It can't be completely crazy." Harry frowned thoughtfully. "Hillis is said to be a brilliant scientist. There has to be a strong purpose behind all this. Otherwise he wouldn't risk his own child in the exchange."

"This exchange," Jeremy said eagerly, "could it work backward?"

"The risks are great . . . but, yes, it could be done. The twinship exists. The one-in-a-million chance was finding an Earth twin in the first place." Harry's eyes narrowed. "But *why*? Why did he risk it?"

"Helene said it was to *help*," Jeremy told him. "At the meeting when she talked to Jessica, they mentioned things like synthetics and hydroponics."

Harry interrupted him. "Those are good things?"

"They all seemed to think they would help Terra," Jeremy said. "Hydroponics is a way of raising plants in water by adding chemicals. Synthetics—well, that's chemicals too. It's making clothes and machines and toys and things out of chemicals."

"That would help us. Our soil is exhausted, and there are too many to feed." Eyes alight, Harry stood up and began pacing up and down the tiny room. "Listen, Jeremy, I don't like Hillis's methods. A feeling of evil comes to me from him. Nevertheless, if he has really found a way to help us to live better here on Terra, how could anyone *not* go along with him? If he is doing good?"

"Good! But he's not good! Everyone in that University has been. . . ." Jeremy fumbled for the word then brought it out, anger lending strength to his voice. *"Damaged!* That's what they said I was because they thought I was one of those kids in the cribs. And everyone is that way—maybe some not as much as others, but everyone's controlled in some way by that Dr. Hillis. They're all like robots. Is that good? You should have seen his face when they held Helene's head and he made her look into his eyes. Afterward she just went all blank."

Harry's face lost its excited expression. "What are you saying?" he demanded in harsh tones. "He forced her to look at him? And there are others too? Jeremy, tell me everything you know about the people inside the University. I must know all about this power of Dr. Hillis's."

Jeremy described in detail the behavior of all those he'd come in contact with at the University, beginning with the young receptionist and her automatic repetition of the phrase "The doctors will help you."

"Of course, the ones who are the worst off are those kids in Total Security." Jeremy's eyes darkened. Even now, in the safety of the barge as it chugged steadily away from the village and the University, it was frightening to think about them. Nevertheless, he described them to Harry.

After he'd finished, Harry sat on the edge of the bunk, staring down at his hands for a long time. Once he clenched and unclenched his fingers and Jeremy heard him groan softly. He was silent for so long that Jeremy became uneasy. Was he still trying to decide whether or not Jeremy was lying, or crazy?

"Harry," he began, and then stopped as Harry raised his head. There was a look of immense sorrow on his face and something else—an unshakable determination. Whatever it was Harry had been thinking about, he had come to a decision.

"He is one of *us*." Harry stood up slowly. "And he has broken the Sacred Law of the Probers. No matter what the results are, it is always wrong to break the Sacred Law, and it is always wrong to injure the innocent. He must be stopped."

Jeremy stared up at him. Harry seemed to have grown bigger. His broad shoulders completely blocked out the light from the little window. Jeremy felt almost afraid to question him.

"These Probers . . . who are they?" he asked at last. "Were you 'probing' when you said things to me in my mind?"

"No!" Harry sounded angry. Then he sighed and rubbed his hand across his forehead. "I'm sorry. I keep forgetting that you don't know. I'll tell you what I can, as much as I'm allowed, about the Probers.

"As you know, here on Terra everyone is telepathic to some extent. It varies from person to person, just like eyesight, or hearing, or the other senses. In children this Greater Sense, as we call it, reaches a peak just before they grow up—in adolescence. Then it tapers off. But once in a while there is a child whose Greater Sense continues to grow. Such a child soon develops a mind that is always open to the thoughts of those around him. The constant battering of his mind makes life miserable for him. I know." Harry smiled a little sadly. "I was a child like that. I couldn't live with my talent. So I was taken by the Probers, others like me, only older. They taught me the secret of the mind shield to keep out the thoughts of others. To protect others from *my* thoughts, however, there is only my voluntary compliance to the Sacred Law."

Jeremy shook his head. Harry hastened to explain.

"Remember when I asked permission to enter your mind?"

Jeremy nodded.

"That is the Sacred Law. A Prober may not enter a mind without freely given permission."

Jeremy began to understand. Helene's permission hadn't been given; he had seen proof of that. And those children in Total Security—no one had asked them, he was sure of it.

"Then the Probers can stop Dr. Hillis?" he asked Harry eagerly. "Can they make those kids normal again?"

"We can stop him," Harry said. "The power of the Probers when they are in unison of thought is too strong for any one person to resist. As for those children, we won't know about them until we can see into their minds." Harry started pacing up and down again. "It will take a little time to get the Probers together, and then perhaps we should make arrangements to meet with the President first and with Senator DeWitt.

"You see, Jeremy, it will not be easy to cut ourselves off from the benefits of your Earth. There will be meetings and committees while they try to figure out some way to punish Hillis and still maintain the contact with your planet. What were those strange things you mentioned?"

"Hydroponics," Jeremy told him. "Synthetics. Lots of other things, too. Television. That's right! I just remembered. That was in the 'secret' message. I don't think Dr. Hillis wanted anyone else to know about it."

"Secret message?"

Jeremy told Harry about the curious way Jessica had concluded her official message to her father, and then continued to talk to him through Helene.

"What is this television?" Harry asked.

Jeremy explained to him as best he could about sound waves and ion particles. Harry listened with a frown on his face. When Jeremy finished up by describing the satellites that encircled the earth to relay live television images to the whole world at the same time, Harry gave a quick nod, his lips set in a thin line.

"That's it," he said. "That's what he wants. He could look into the eyes of everyone on Terra at once. Think of that, Jeremy—a whole world of people controlled by Dr. Hillis. They'd be like those children in there, or like the workers and the guards, with just enough wit left to do his bidding."

Harry jumped up, smacking his fist into his palm. "The bridge to Earth must be broken, even if it means giving up all those benefits. The thing is, if we stop Hillis and he has already learned the secret of this television, sooner or later some other power-seeking Prober will come along and

145*

use it. Thoughts cannot be lost or hidden for too long on Terra. We must act fast!"

"I'll help you," Jeremy said eagerly, "any way I can."

Harry walked over to the window. "We must stop that message tomorrow. There won't be time to form committees . . . though perhaps I can get to DeWitt. . . ." Harry's voice trailed off and he seemed to be speaking to himself, forgetful of Jeremy, until Jeremy went over and put a hand on his arm.

"I'll go with you and help," he repeated.

"What? Oh, but you can't come with me. It's too dangerous."

"Dangerous! But I've already been there. I can show you where to go. I can—"

Harry shook his head. "No, you can't come. I have to meet him alone—or better, with as many Probers as I can summon quickly. We'll take care of him our way."

He paused and stared at something outside. Jeremy followed his gaze. Several miles away on the end of the east arm of the harbor was Old Fort. Right at this moment the fort was framed in the exact center of the little porthole window. Jeremy remembered what Harry had called it: "the Hillis stronghold." In his mind the evil swirling around the image of the doctor grew. A whole world at stake. . . .

"You're right," he said slowly. "The important thing is to stop the message. Helene and I can wait to get home."

"About your going home. . . ." Harry didn't look at him and his voice was curiously gentle. "Don't count on that, Jeremy. I am not at all sure now that an exchange would work again."

146*

14*

"*But you* said!" Jeremy cried. "*You said it could be done.*"
He started shaking Harry's arm.

"I meant that *in theory* it would work. But both parties
to the exchange have to be willing, or one of the parties
has to be strong enough to force the other to exchange. And
Jessica wouldn't be willing, not yet. Another thing is that
your cousin's mind is no longer the way it was when she
came here."

Jeremy felt something cold clutch at his stomach. "You
mean he's making her like those kids in the cribs?"

"Each time she is forced to make contact with Jessica,
her telepathic powers grow less, and so does her will. Perhaps that is how those children became as they are. He
was searching for another Earth twin, someone else besides
his own daughter. He forced them and forced them until
they lost their will. Now their empty minds will be used
as . . . as *receptacles*. Your cousin is not like that yet. But
her mind is not as strong as it was when the exchange was
first made. And, Jeremy, think of this: Jessica must have
been very strong to have forced your cousin to leave her
home and come here."

"Maybe she didn't have to force her," Jeremy said slowly.
"I think Helene was ready to go anywhere."

"Nevertheless, you can't risk it, because once you start

to make the exchange, you have to finish it. Otherwise. . . ." He shrugged.

"Otherwise what?" Jeremy demanded.

"There is only one outcome for an unsuccessful exchange: death by dissolution. You and your cousin and Jessica would become scattered bits of energy, lost in the great void of space." Harry made a wide gesture with both arms.

The void of space. It made Jeremy dizzy to try to imagine it. "But," he began, his voice lacking conviction even to himself, "it worked once."

"No." Harry was firm. "You and your cousin do not equal Jessica. I think she will be a Prober like her father." He smiled tiredly at Jeremy. "I suppose if you didn't oppose me on this, Jeremy, I'd wonder where your guts were. All along you've shown a great deal of enterprise, I'm well aware of that. And that's just why I have to protect you now."

Once more Harry turned to the window, where the sky outside was reddening with a sunset glow. "Soon the yeomen will be finished with the oyster beds," he said. "I'm going to tell them that we need rowing practice and that we must go back to the harbor in the dinghies. We'll leave the barge out here. We've done it before and it won't attract any attention. I'm going to leave you on the barge."

"What!" Jeremy started instinctively for the door, but Harry caught his arm.

"To protect you," he said quietly. "And there's something else, Jeremy. I have a big job to do. I am convinced that nothing from Earth is good for us. Terra must go at its own

148*

pace. But I may have a hard time convincing others of that. I can't have you on my mind too." The big man suddenly looked less sure of himself. Jeremy's words of protest died on his lips. He sat exhausted on the bunk.

"There's nothing more I can say, is there." It was a statement.

"I'm sorry," Harry said. Jeremy could feel him looking down at him, but he did not look up. "There's food in the ice chest," Harry said. "Try to rest. I'll be back tomorrow, or somebody will—in case I can't make it."

He might not win. There was a chance of that. Slowly Jeremy's head came up. "Thanks, Harry," he said. "And— good luck."

Harry smiled and clapped him on the shoulder; then he was gone.

Outside, the boys had started to come back to the barge. Jeremy could hear them laughing and talking as they put away their gear. In a moment he heard Harry telling them about the change in plans. Groans of protest followed, but there was no serious argument. Apparently the yeomen were always ready to accept Harry's judgments. Didn't they wonder what had happened to *him*? They'd all seen him and been curious about him. Didn't they guess that there was a prisoner in the cabin? For once more Jeremy knew that was what he was. He sank back on the bunk and shut his eyes.

Soon the clop-clopping of the oars died away and it was quiet. Jeremy could hear the soft lapping of the waves against the side of the barge. He was alone. There was no way to get back to the village; it was at least three miles from here. He tossed his head restlessly on the hard pillow. Would he have to stay on Terra forever? Harry thought so. Over and over, Jeremy's thoughts traveled the same path. Nothing to be done . . . nothing. Against his will, his eyes began to close as the gentle up and down motion of the barge lulled his tired body. Still telling himself that there had to be a way out, Jeremy fell asleep.

When he awoke it was dark. Strange, he thought, his bed was moving, rocking. Then he remembered and sat up. How long had he slept? Stumbling to the door, he stepped out onto the deck of the barge.

The night air was cool and fresh. Above him stars pinpointed familiar constellations. Looking at them, Jeremy was gripped again by the now frequent feeling of disbelief. How *could* there be another world so like his own that even the same stars shone above it? Not just a world then, but a universe . . . a cosmos. It was too big to think about.

Jeremy took a firm grip on the handrail and walked around to the opposite side of the barge. He was looking toward Connecticut. On his left, at the tip of the western land arm of the harbor, a white beam flashed intermittently from the lighthouse, just the way it did at home. He looked in the opposite direction. On the eastern arm a blocky building was plainly floodlighted. Old Fort. At home it wasn't lit up at night. But then at home it was a museum piece; here it was still a fort in a very real sense. A fort, barricaded and guarded against trespassers. Jeremy glared his hatred across the dark water that lay between him and the Hillis stronghold. Was the doctor sleeping now, secure in his coming seizure of power? Jeremy drummed his fingers on the handrail.

Sleep had restored his energy. Now he regretted not pushing his arguments with Harry. He should be with him, he thought, not only to help him, but also to use the opportunity to try to get home. Harry *had* to be wrong about Helene; there *had* to be a way to reverse the procedure that had brought them to Terra. But instead of trying, here he was, a useless prisoner. Jeremy put his head down on the rail and shut his eyes.

Suddenly into the emptiness of his mind came a whisper of thought that was not his own. Raising his head, he stared out across the black water toward Old Fort. Someone over there was calling to him for help!

It was like pushing through curtains of fog to catch the thought clearly. Mixed with the call was a longing for home, for the presence of people and things that Jeremy knew too. His heart began to race. Dr. Robertson had guessed that animals might be telepathic. . . . Why couldn't it be Charlie?

Fixing his eyes firmly on the dark outline of the fort, he willed a message toward it: *I'm coming.* In a moment the pressure of the other thought diminished and Jeremy relaxed too.

Between the barge and the fort lay about two miles of water. He'd swum a mile and a half once. From the ball field to the dock at home was exactly that, and everyone tried it at least once. Only, of course, out here in the Sound, you wouldn't have the comfort of knowing that a few strokes toward shore would give you a firm toehold in the rocky bottom. But then, last summer when he'd made the swim from the ball field he'd only needed a toehold once. Jeremy countered each of his own objections as he moved along the rail to the opening where a rope ladder dangled down to the water. Of course it was nighttime now . . . but he'd swim toward the light and it wouldn't seem so dark.

Hand over hand, he went down and in a moment slipped quietly into the water. Along the surface it was still faintly warm from the sun, and for a while he swam along effortlessly. Occasionally, however, one of his legs dropped down into the chill of deeper water and he was reminded of the depths beneath him. Each time, he pulled his leg up and struck out more strongly toward his goal.

It wasn't until he was almost halfway across that something occurred to him. Suppose it hadn't been Charlie calling to him? Suppose the reason the identity of the caller was so uncertain was that it was not someone he knew at all, but Dr. Hillis?

He hesitated a moment, almost afraid to test it; then he sent out a call to the fort. There was no response of any kind.

15

Now both legs scissored down into the cold. *I must float,* Jeremy thought, as he fought back panic. Turning over on his back, he forced himself to take slow, deep breaths. That was better; soon he was able to turn his head and look around him. Back of him lay the barge, looking much smaller than it had. Ahead was Old Fort, nearer now but still impossibly far. *I'll never make it,* he thought, and his legs automatically stiffened and began to sink.

Against the lighter bulk of the fort was a tall vertical shaft. At first he'd thought it was part of the building itself, but now he suddenly realized that it was moving up and down. It was the channel buoy, not clanging the way it did at home, but there just the same, anchored firmly to the bottom of the Sound. It was the toehold he needed. He swam toward it.

Jeremy rested on the buoy until his breathing was normal again. Then he struck out once more for Old Fort. Soon he could make out a tall wall encircling the land side of the compound. The wall stopped partway out on the end of the point; apparently here the giant boulders that extended into the water were considered barrier enough. By swimming out a bit farther Jeremy was able to avoid the wall.

A few moments more, and he was picking his way between the boulders into the shallows. When he reached the beach he stopped and listened. No sound, except the water sloshing between the rocks. He walked on toward the fort. As he drew near, he heard the tread of measured footsteps somewhere above him. Looking up, Jeremy saw a man walking along the parapet on the second floor of the fort. Quickly he slipped into the shadow of the wall and waited for the man to pass. But now the footsteps seemed to quicken, or was it that there were more of them? Edging out from the side of the building, Jeremy looked up. Two University guards were approaching each other on the parapet. The rifles on their shoulders threw long shadows onto the wall behind them.

"Check."

"Check."

Their monotone voices sent a shiver down Jeremy's back. He flattened himself against the wall until they were well gone.

And now the call came again—from within the fort. Years of visiting the place at home had made Jeremy familiar with the layout of the fort. He only hoped they hadn't changed it too much. He ran along next to the wall to where there should be a narrow stairway going up. There was. Upstairs he saw the same long narrow openings leading through yard-thick masonry into the second floor. The problem was, which one to enter? Jeremy closed his eyes briefly to concentrate on the direction of the still-urgent call. Then he ran toward a door on his right and quickly slipped inside.

Instead of an empty, dusty storage room he was in a narrow hallway with a closed door facing him. Hearing the guards' footsteps returning, he thrust himself hurriedly against the door. He fell forward into a softly lighted room.

Paneled in dark, polished wood, the room was set about with great pots of greenery and hung with gilt birdcages much the way the anteroom to the auditorium was. Here, instead of bricks, there was a soft gold-colored carpeting on the floor. Jeremy was glad of its luxurious depth as he sped noiselessly across it to an opening he had spied at the far end. Another hall and more doors. He hesitated for only a moment and then ran toward one of them.

The knob of the door turned easily in Jeremy's hand, but the door would not open. He pushed harder and felt it give slightly. Something was holding it back on the other side. Jeremy rammed his shoulder against it, and now a quarter of an inch of space appeared at the molding.

"Go away," a small voice told him.

Jeremy could hear the guards' voices outside and he didn't have time to stop and wonder what Helene was doing here.

"Open the door," he whispered. "It's me, Jeremy."

Something was dragged slowly on the floor in the room beyond, and then the door opened just enough to let Jeremy slip inside. The cousins stared at each other. Helene was a mess, red-eyed and disheveled; she looked as if she had been fighting.

"What are you doing here?" she demanded, but even though her chin came up in the old snippy way, Helene's voice had lost its sharpness.

"What are you . . ." Jeremy began, and then ran past her. Charlie lay on the bed behind Helene. He picked him up and held him close to his chest.

"He's eaten something for *me*," Helene told him rather smugly. "When they found him in the University he was sort of worn out and limp. Dr. Robertson said he wouldn't survive in a cage . . . so they brought him here. Dr. Hillis said there's something special about him that he wants to . . . to study further. Poor Charlie." Her eyes darkened and she was silent. Then she looked down. "Jeremy, look what you've done. You're dripping all over the floor. What a mess!"

"Oh, Helene!" Jeremy wanted to shake her. "What's the matter with you? Who cares about floors. We're in the biggest mess there ever was!"

Helene's face suddenly crumpled. "I know it!" she wailed. "Oh, Jeremy, I know it! Dr. Hillis is coming here tonight. He said he can't wait until tomorrow to talk to Jessica. I'm scared!" Twisting her fingers in her skirt, Helene turned away from him. "That's why I tried to call you," she said in a low voice.

"*You* called me?" He'd been so sure it was Charlie; it had felt like Charlie. But if it was Helene, that changed everything. "Helene," he said, "do you want to go home now?"

"Home?" She shrugged. "It's better than here anyhow. Better than being a robot."

"It could be a lot better," Jeremy said, bending his head over the cat. "Maybe we were both . . . not very nice. Maybe we could be, well, nicer," he finished awkwardly.

There was a silence, and then he heard Helene sigh. "Well, maybe. But what's the use of thinking about it—home, I mean? I think we're stuck here forever."

"There is a way to get home. We could work the exchange backward. If you want to do it, it will work—as long as you still don't think Dr. Hillis is God or somebody, the way you did at the meeting this morning." Helene looked surprised. "I was there. And it's all a lot worse than you know." Briefly Jeremy told Helene all he'd learned at the University and from Harry.

"But Dr. Hillis is coming here *tonight*," Helene cried. "Your friend will be too late!"

They stared at each other. Finally Helene nodded.

"Yes, I'll try it," she whispered.

"We'll stand close together. I'll hold Charlie. We have to concentrate very hard on wanting to go home, no matter what Jessica wants. OK? Then when I say 'Now,' we'll. . . ."

Jeremy stopped. Outside the building there was a sound of voices. He ran to the window. On the road from the village he saw a moving stream of bobbing lights coming toward the fort. A moment more, and he could make out some of the people holding the torches.

"Helene!" he cried. "It's Harry . . . and Senator De-Witt!"

On either side of Harry were two older men, none of them as tall as the fisherman, but all with the same proud bearing. Probers, Jeremy guessed. Under one of the torches he saw another familiar face: the sleeping girl from Total Security who had reminded him of Jane Albert. She was awake now and waving her torch about excitedly. Behind her were other boys and girls—hundreds of them, it seemed.

"The kids," Jeremy said softly. "Harry got to the kids." He wanted to shout or laugh. "It's all right now, Helene."

"No, I'm afraid it's not. Not quite yet," said a steely voice behind them.

Helene and Jeremy spun around to see Dr. Hillis standing in the doorway. They watched in horror as he shut the door behind him. Jeremy heard the lock click.

"Don't look at him," he cried, grabbing Helene's hand with his free one.

"Yes, you will look at me," Dr. Hillis said quietly. "And you will receive one more message from Earth. It is all I need. No matter what *they*"—he jerked his head toward the window—"do now, I will have the secret of television and somehow, someday, I will use it." His eyes shone.

"Remember what we said," Jeremy cried. "Do it now, Helene, *now!*"

Helene's head swung around and their eyes met.

"Home," Jeremy whispered. There was a click behind his eyes and a sudden feeling of dizziness.

"It won't work," he heard Dr. Hillis say from far away. The doctor began to laugh. At first the laughter was as distant as his voice; then it gained in strength. A moment more and the dizziness left Jeremy.

"It didn't work," he said dully. "We're not strong enough."

"Of course you're not. Don't try it again or you'll end up nowhere. You understand about the dissolution?" Dr. Hillis narrowed his eyes as he spoke to Jeremy. Then he walked over to the window and looked out. "We'll need as much time as possible," he said. He went back to the door and began shoving the chest of drawers in front of it.

Jeremy was clutching Charlie so tightly that he began to howl. Charlie was afraid, terribly afraid—and Jeremy could *feel* the current of fear flow directly into his own mind.

"Once more," he whispered to Helene. "Don't be afraid. This time it will work!"

There was an answering pressure from Helene's hand as Jeremy felt her mind join his. *Now*, he thought. . . .

"Kitty-kitty-kitty-kitty . . ." he murmured. Charlie had to think of home, had to want to go there. . . . And as he concentrated on that, Jeremy's head was suddenly filled with the force of Charlie's longing.

This time, when the click came, the descent into vertigo was immediate. The room swiftly faded away behind a swirling mist of light and dark specks. Someone on the other side was resisting them, but they were stronger, stronger. . . . It was Jeremy's last coherent thought before the sickening cold of space took over.

For a long moment Jeremy ceased to exist. Then there was a sudden brighter sparkle of light, a shock of physical impact, and it was over.

He and Helene and Charlie were in the kitchen at home.

"We made it!" Jeremy heard Helene say. He nodded, still too dazed for speech. Charlie jumped out of his arms, and for a few seconds the only sound was the soft tick-ticking of his claws as he walked toward the pantry.

"It was Charlie, wasn't it? He gave us the extra strength." Helene was staring at the cat.

Jeremy released her hand and pointed at the table. On it was a jar of peanut butter, a Coke, a loaf of bread, and several volumes of encyclopedias. Jeremy touched the bread with the tip of one finger. Just a moment ago, Jessica had stood here. Quickly he withdrew his hand.

159*

"We did give them one thing, you know," he said slowly.

"We did?"

"The bread wrapper, remember? They'll figure out how to make plastics from that."

"That's right," Helene said. "They can make dishes and rain hats. . . ."

"Machine parts," Jeremy put in. "Furniture."

A little smile began on Helene's face. "Barbie dolls. Silly Putty." Jeremy smiled back.

At the door to the pantry Charlie growled softly. Eyes on Jeremy, he arched his back against the door.

"You *bet* it's dinnertime," Jeremy told him. He went to the shelf in the pantry where the cat food was kept. After opening a can of it, he carried it out to the back porch where Charlie's dish and water bowl still sat on the floor. For a moment Jeremy watched as Charlie attacked his food hungrily; then he walked over to the edge of the porch. Leaning on the railing, he looked at the sky. Overhead the stars were bright.

Endless reaches of stars. Jeremy stared up at them, unaware of Helene's presence until she spoke.

"Each star is a sun," she said. "And each sun might have planets around it. I wonder which sun is Terra's."

Jeremy shook his head. "None of those," he said. "Some place—beyond our stars. We'll never know. The bridge is broken and it might be thousands of years before there's another one. Maybe by then it will work better."

They looked up in silence for a while and then Jeremy turned around.

"Come on," he said. "Let's tell them we're home."